THE SLEEPOVER GANG

Louise   Jo   Charlie   Alex

Alex can't wait to get her friends to her cabin in
the woods.

Jo is fascinated by Alex's strange story of Jake and
the girl he meets in the snow.

Charlie can't believe anyone lives so far from
civilisation.

Louise is terrified of wolves and werewolves but she
can't resist Alex's story.

The Snowed-In
Sleepover

Sharon Siamon

Hodder
Children's
Books

a division of Hodder Headline plc

To Becky

First published in Great Britain in 1997
by Hodder Children's Books

10 9 8 7 6 5

A CIP catalogue record for this book is available
from the British Library

ISBN 0 340 67277 3

Typeset by Palimpsest Book Production Limited,
Polmont, Stirlingshire

Printed and bound in Great Britain by
Clays Ltd, St Ives plc

Hodder Children's Books
a division of Hodder Headline plc
338 Euston Road
London NW1 3BH

One

'What on earth is that horrible noise!' Alex's father shouted.

'It's *music*!' came a chorus of voices from the back seat. Alex and her friends Jo, Charlie and Louise had just turned up the sound on their favourite CD.

'Well, it sounds like wolves howling. Can you turn it down so I can hear the weather forecast?' Alex's dad roared. 'I want to know if it's snowing in the mountains.'

Alex shrugged and flicked off her portable CD player. The trip seemed endless to the four girls. They were packed in the back seat of the jeep like sardines. Behind them were ski equipment, snowshoes, sleeping bags and bags of food for their weekend at Alex's mountain cabin.

Alex gazed out of the window. The scenery looked so different in winter, but she was starting to recognise familiar landmarks.

1

'We're getting close,' she cried. 'We've almost reached the land of snow, sleepovers and great spooky stories! Did I tell you the cabin is part of an old gold mine?'

'Only about a hundred times,' Jo laughed. The four of them had been talking about this trip for weeks.

In the front seat, Alex's mother searched for a weather report on the radio. Suddenly, the clear voice of a newscaster cut through the static:

'A student worker was killed by wolves today at the Woodlands Forest Preserve. The body of the young woman was discovered with five wolves circling it in a large pen where she was conducting wolf research. It is the first documented killing of a human being by timber wolves in North America. All five of the animals were destroyed.'

The four friends turned horrified faces to each other.

'What a way to die!' Charlie shuddered. 'Imagine being torn apart by wolves!'

Jo's blue eyes were huge. 'Didn't you say people had seen wolves, up near your camp?' Jo asked Alex.

2

'We hear lots of stories,' Alex nodded. 'But we've never actually seen a wolf. They usually keep away from people.'

Louise clutched Alex's arm. 'You never told us there were wolves,' she said, her face pale. Of all of them, Louise had looked forward to this weekend the least. She liked to stay cosily indoors during the winter. The thought of a cold, lonely mountain cabin was not appealing. And now – wolves!

The radio was forecasting more snow. Charlie wriggled restlessly in her cramped position against the window. 'I've never seen so much snow in my life!' she cried. 'How can there be *more*?'

In another hour they had reached the lower slopes of the mountains. Now the road snaked up between towering cliffs of black rock.

'Not much farther.' Alex shook her tangled curls out of her eyes, and sat up straight. 'Can we stop at the Crossroads Store?' she called out to her parents in the front seat.

'There's a store? Here?' Charlie wriggled her way forward to peer hopefully out of the front window of the jeep.

'It's just ahead, at the crossroads!' Alex

3

told her. 'Bell's Store sells everything. Groceries and gas and tons of junk food for you, Charlie.' Charlie loved to eat.

Alex's father shook his head. 'There's absolutely no reason to stop! This time, I didn't forget a thing.'

'Did you bring breakfast cereal?' Alex asked.

'*Both* your favourite kinds.'

'Bottled water?'

'Ten litres.'

'Bacon?'

'A kilo! . . . I told you, I thought of everything we'd need for the entire week-end.'

'How about chemicals, for the toilet?'

'Naturally.'

'A can opener that works without electricity?'

'Of course . . .'

'I know,' Alex cried. 'Matches, for the woodstove.'

'I brought five hundred matches.'

Alex's mother broke in. 'Why don't you stop, Bert?' she suggested. 'The girls are dying to visit the store, and there must be something we need. There always is, you know.'

Alex's father banged on the steering

4

wheel. 'This time, I'm telling you, I've thought of everything.' He stepped on the gas and breezed right past the little grey building with its cheerful sign, *Bell's Country Store*. The jeep turned right at the crossroads and sped up the steep mountain road.

'The sooner we get there,' Alex's father sang out, 'the sooner we can start having fun!'

Half an hour later the four friends stood in the snowy road and watched the green jeep drive away down the mountain. Behind them, the little log cabin stood almost buried in snow. Smoke trickled from the chimney, but the windows were dark.

'So . . .' Jo broke the silence. 'Your dad forgot the lantern fuel.'

Alex sighed. 'Good old Dad with his, "I've got *everything* we need." Everything except lantern fuel. We wouldn't have much fun tonight with no light.' She closed the iron gate that stretched across the road. It had a rusty sign that read: Hook Mountain Gold Mine.

'Oh, I think we would have tons of fun.' Charlie spun in a circle on the snow-packed road. Her smooth black hair was tucked into the hood of her bright red parka and her eyes sparkled. 'I think it would be great if your parents didn't come back at all. We could have the whole cabin to ourselves. We could get the fire roaring and stay up late, and eat . . .' She spun around again, arms outstretched like a skater.

'. . . and tell stories,' Jo added. 'Really terrifying stories about being stranded in a lonely cabin on the top of a mountain . . . with wolves pacing back and forth outside.' Jo loved scary stories.

'Stop!' Louise clamped her blue ski mitts over her ears.

'Stories later,' Charlie laughed. 'Right now, let's have fun with all this snow!' Charlie plunged into the deep snowdrift at the side of the road. She tried to throw a snowball at Jo, but the snow was too cold and dry to stick together. Her snowball burst in the air, dusting Jo with shining flakes.

'Missed me,' Jo laughed.

'Watch me do a perfect front flip!' Alex cried, launching her body into the air, and landing beside Charlie. 'Whoo. It's like landing on a cloud.' Alex loved tumbling and juggling and all the circus arts.

'The pine trees look like women in long white gowns.' Louise reached for a snow-covered pine branch.

'Louise, no!' Alex shrieked. 'You'll start an avalanche!'

Too late. The moment Louise touched the branch, the whole mass of white snow showered around her head.

'I'll help you,' Jo laughed, wading through the thigh-deep drift to rescue Louise.

'Me too!' shouted Charlie.

The next thing they knew, they were all laughing, and rolling in the snow, trying to get up, getting stuck, and flopping over again. Finally they lay back, panting, letting the snowflakes fall and melt on their tongues and eyelashes.

'It's so quiet.' Jo stared up at the snowy forest. 'But I get a feeling that something happened here. It's almost like an echo . . .'

Suddenly, the silence was broken by a distant howl that froze them for an instant, unable to move. Then Charlie jumped up and threw back her snowy hood. 'Listen. What was that?'

Before she finished speaking, the howling came again. It was a sound that sent shivers down the insides of their warm ski clothes and into their snowboots.

7

'They're wolves,' Alex scrambled to her feet. 'We heard them this summer.'

'Wolves!' Louise screamed, struggling to get up. Her face was white.

'Take it easy.' Alex reached out a hand to help Louise to her feet. 'They're still a long way from here. But maybe we should go inside.'

'After what happened to that poor girl,' Jo agreed, leading the way up the path to the cabin door, 'I don't think we should take any chances with wolves.'

Two

'Before we go inside,' Alex shouted, 'everybody grab an armload of wood for the stove.'

They raced round the corner of the cabin to the wood pile, gathered armloads of firewood and staggered back to dump it in the woodbox, just inside the cabin door.

Alex banged the door shut and latched it behind them. 'That should keep the wolves out,' she panted. 'And we've got enough wood to last until Mum and Dad get back.'

Louise looked miserably at Alex. 'Why did your mum have to go to the store with your dad?'

Alex patted Louise's arm. 'You don't know Dad. Once he started talking to the Bells, down at the store, we wouldn't see him till midnight unless Mum was there to pry him loose. Mr Bell tells the best stories . . .' Alex shook her head.

'What kind of stories?' Jo asked.

'Everything from old legends to the latest Crossroads gossip,' Alex laughed. Sooner or later, everyone ends up at the Bell's store to buy something. So Mr Bell can tell you who caught the best fish, who shot the biggest moose, who discovered gold . . .' She paused. 'He told us an amazing story about the people who had the cabin before us. Of course, it can't all be true.'

'What did he tell you?' Jo pressed her.

'They were gold prospectors, a family named Kingston. They had a son, a bit older than we are, named Jake. He was tall and dark, and played the guitar . . .' Alex's eyes crinkled up with laughter. 'I hope *that* part of the story is true.'

'He sounds great,' Jo agreed. 'What else?'

'The Kingstons found gold, Mr Bell told us. But then something happened and they suddenly shut the place down and disappeared, six years ago.'

'Weird,' Jo said. 'No wonder the cabin has this deserted feeling.'

The others turned and stared around the little log building. They'd been so busy running back and forth unloading the jeep that they hadn't really looked at it closely.

'It's dark in here,' Louise shivered. 'The

windows are so small!' She was right. The corners of the cabin were filled with shadows. In one corner, a ladder disappeared up into a dark sleeping-loft.

'That's why we need the lanterns, even in the afternoon,' Alex agreed. She gathered up a few sticks of stove wood. 'If we had big windows, all the heat from the stove would escape.'

The round wood stove stood in the very centre of the cabin floor. Alex opened the glass doors and pitched in another log. There was a hiss and crackle as it blazed into life.

'I love the smell of a wood fire,' Jo sighed. 'Let's set up our sleeping bags around the stove. Then you can tell us all about the Kingstons, and their son, Jake.'

'First, let's break out the junk food,' Charlie reminded them.

'Do you think there are any candles,' Louise asked. 'In case it gets really dark . . .?'

'We didn't bring candles because Dad *thought of everything*,' Alex laughed. 'But there might be some in the kitchen cupboards.'

They searched carefully, but found only four short ends of candles in the back of a drawer.

'Maybe there are some more in this

box . . .' Alex dragged a flat metal box out from under a shelf. She carried it over to the stove and sat down cross-legged in front of the fire.

As she pried open the lid, the others leaned forward to see what was inside.

There were no candles.

On top of a heap of papers was a jagged piece of rock, like a paper weight. Alex held it up to the firelight. Her eyes lit with excitement. 'This is gold ore, I'm sure,' she cried. 'Mr Bell told us what to look for.' She pointed to some yellow streaks. 'See here? This is gold.'

Charlie reached for the lump of rock from Alex's hand. 'Hey . . . real gold! What else is in the box?'

'Some notebooks and papers . . . and this.' Alex held up a small black journal. She cracked open the covers. They were stiff from being damp and then dried out again. 'It's some kind of record,' she said. 'With dates and everything. But what horrible handwriting! I can hardly read it.'

'Here,' Charlie said. 'Let's light a candle with one of your dad's five hundred matches.'

Jo peered over Alex's shoulder. 'There's a name on one of the notebooks. It looks like . . . *Jake Kingston*,' Jo read.

Alex looked excitedly from one to the other. 'These must be Jake's school notebooks. He had to take classes by correspondence because he lived so far from a school.' Alex flipped through the pages of the small black book. 'This is some kind of personal journal. Look here . . .' She held the first page up to the candlelight. 'It says,

Wed. Feb. 1
I don't trust Digger. I'm going to start writing things down, in case I need proof, later . . .'

'Wow!' Alex sat back. Her eyebrows were raised so high they disappeared under her curls. 'Spooky!'

'What?' Jo urged. 'Why are you looking like that, Alex? Who was Digger?'

Alex shook her head wonderingly. 'Digger was the Kingstons' partner in the gold mine. Mr Bell told us some terrible things about him . . . but maybe they're true.'

'What did he say?' Jo urged.

'This is a long story,' Alex said, 'and it's cold sitting on the floor. Let's pull the couch and chair over by the stove and spread out our sleeping bags on top.'

'And break out the junk food,' Charlie reminded them again.

13

They were suddenly all ravenous. While Jo and Alex dragged the heavy pine furniture up to the stove, Charlie and Louise pawed through the bags of food, finding potato chips, chocolate cookies, granola bars, cheese and crackers.

'It's a little on the health-foody side,' Charlie sighed, as she bit into a granola bar. 'But considering it was your dad who packed, Alex, it could be a lot worse.'

'Speaking of your dad,' Louise glanced nervously at Alex, 'when do you think they'll be back?'

They were all quiet for a moment, listening for the sound of the jeep coming up the mountain, for footsteps crunching on the snow outside. Without saying so, they were also listening for the howling of the wolves.

But there was only the crackle of the fire, and the crunch of Charlie's granola bar.

'It hasn't been that long,' Alex said.

'Well, I wish they'd hurry up,' Louise looked anxiously at the small window. 'Now it's getting dark outside.'

Three

Jo, Louise and Charlie settled themselves on the comfortable old couch. Alex sank into the armchair in front of the fire with the box on her lap. Their goose-down sleeping bags surrounded them like light, soft arms.

'And now I'll tell you what Mr Bell told us about Jake, and Digger,' Alex said.

'At least it's not a wolf story,' Louise shuddered.

Alex's eyebrows shot up again. 'But he *did* tell us about wolves . . .' she warned. 'That's how the stories about Digger got started.'

Charlie's eyes danced. 'Come on, Louise, what do you expect? Don't you know it's February – the month of werewolves?'

'Stop teasing, Charlie. You're interrupting my story.' Alex shook her curly head. 'Let's see if I can remember . . . how did it start?'

They sat, watching the firelight flicker

15

across Alex's freckled face as she began to tell the story.

Alex had a crisp, no-nonsense voice that made everything she said sound true. She began to speak in her clear, matter-of-fact way.

It started about six winters ago, when Digger Grimes began to kill the wolves.

Digger was a partner in the Kingstons' Hook Mountain Gold Mine. He looked after all the drilling and blasting and digging tunnels. That's how he got his nickname, 'Digger'.

Jake Kingston didn't like him. There was something evil about Digger. He loved machinery, but seemed to like to hurt and torture living things. On top of that, Digger teased Jake about playing the guitar, and called him a sissy. When he tried to talk to his parents, they reminded him they couldn't run the mine without Digger's skill.

'We don't have to like him,' Jake's father said. 'We need him. He's the best mining engineer we could get on short notice, and he's a wizard with engines.'

Nobody around the Crossroads liked Digger much, either. He was mean and short and smelly. He drank too much rum and kicked the dogs that hung around the country store. He shot at the ravens that came around looking for scraps. And then he started setting traps for the wolves.

The people around here didn't mind wolves. They seemed like part of the mountains and the forest, and they rarely bothered anyone. Wolves didn't raid garbage, like the bears. They howled at the moon when the moon was full, and people got used to the sound.

But Digger hated the wolves, and feared them. He had heard old French legends of the *loup-garou*, the werewolf, and he had it fixed in his mind that a special werewolf was haunting the Hook Mountain Mine.

This werewolf had once been a prospector named Willie Low. When Willie struck it rich on the mountain, he went crazy with greed. All he cared about was gold and he worked his miners to death to get it. Two men were killed when a tunnel collapsed on them.

That day, Willie disappeared without a trace. People whispered he had been attacked by wolves, and was now a werewolf himself.

Digger was sure that Willie Low, the

werewolf, was prowling around the mine with the wolves, waiting to devour anyone working in his old mine. He started putting out poison meat for the wolves. They were too smart to eat it, but a couple of families lost their dogs. Then Digger set leghold traps for the wolves. These traps could destroy an animal's leg with one snap of their cruel, terrible teeth.

One day in early February, he and Jake were in the store. Digger was buying meat, to bait his wolf traps.

'You'd better watch what you catch in those traps,' Mr Bell told Digger.

'That's none of your business,' Digger growled.

'It will be my business if you catch my dog,' Mr Bell told him.

'You keep your dog away from the mine.' Digger's face got all red. 'And stay away yourself.' He plunked down his money and stormed out of the store without another word.

Jake apologised for Digger. 'He's got this thing about wolves . . .' he shrugged. 'He wants to kill them all.'

'What does your dad say?' Mr Bell leaned his elbows on the counter and looked at Jake.

'Oh . . . Dad,' Jake shuffled his feet and looked down at the floor. 'He's pretty busy. They're putting down another drill hole.' Both Jake's parents were geologists. What Jake wasn't saying, but what everybody knew, was that the partners were almost out of money. If they didn't find gold soon, they'd be bust.

'Well, you'd better tell your dad to get a grip on that Digger,' Mr Bell warned. 'He's getting pretty unpopular around here.'

'I'll tell him.' Jake looked miserable, and Mr Bell felt a little sorry for him.

'And remember,' he said, leaning over the counter to pat Jake's arm, 'you people aren't the first ones to lose your shirts looking for gold on Hook Mountain. Prospectors have been digging around up there since I was a kid, and my dad ran this store.'

'I know.' Jake looked even more miserable. 'We keep breaking into their old tunnels.'

'Well, maybe you'll be the ones that make the big strike.' Mr Bell shook his head. 'With gold, you just never know.' He offered Jake a jelly worm out of a jar on the counter. 'Fifty years ago, Willie Low was ready to give up, and he threw down his rock hammer in disgust. It hit a rock, and stripped the moss

19

off the biggest seam of gold this country has ever seen!'

'Yeah, I know, Mr Bell. I've heard all the stories. Our big strike is just over the next ridge, down the next drill hole.'

'Well, it's out there somewhere, son.'

'So why aren't you up in the mountains, drilling, and blasting and hauling rock in the freezing cold?' Jake asked.

'Because I can get rich, just standing here in my nice warm store, selling food and gas to guys like you,' Mr Bell laughed.

'You mean, to fools like us,' Jake said.

There was the muffled roar of a dynamite blast. 'I'd better get back up there,' Jake turned to go. 'I'll talk to Dad about Digger.'

But Jake never had a chance to talk to his dad. That dynamite blast opened up a new seam of gold. Jake's parents left the same day to take gold samples to test in the lab down in the city.

They left Jake with Digger, their trusted partner.

'Not good!' Louise shuddered, twisting a strand of her fair hair. 'How could they leave him alone with that horrible man?'

'That part we saw in the journal, where he

said *I don't trust Digger*,' Jo cried. 'Maybe he wrote that when his parents went away.'

'Read some more,' Charlie begged.

'OK.' Alex cracked open the stiff cover of the notebook. 'I wish his handwriting wasn't so awful!' She leaned closer to the candle to read.

'Thursday, Feb. 2
I talked to Digger and told him what Mr Bell said about the wolves. Digger is definitely getting weird. I catch him staring at me with a funny crooked squint that gives me shivers. And he has some crazy notion that there's a werewolf on Hook Mountain. He claims to have seen a huge white beast on the night of the full moon. He thinks it's after him . . .'

'What exactly is a w-werewolf?' Louise stammered. 'A person who turns into a wolf?'

'Just at night,' Charlie said. 'By day they're as normal as you or me,' She pushed her upper lip up over her teeth. 'But you can always tell by their fangs – these two, long pointy teeth.'

As if on cue, a long, quavering howl came from the forest. It was such a lonely sound, a hungry sound, that even Charlie stopped to listen.

'They're getting closer,' Louise whispered, pulling the sleeping bag around her ears. 'I hate that sound.'

Another howl answered the first, and then another, and another, until the howling ringed the cabin.

They clutched each other's arms as they listened in the dark cabin to the fearful chorus outside.

Four

The chorus of wolf howls died away at last.

'They've gone,' Jo sighed.

'I don't think so,' Louise whispered. 'I think they're waiting just outside the door.'

'I'll take a look,' Charlie said. She jumped up and scratched a peephole in the frost-covered window. 'I don't see any wolves,' she told them. 'But it's getting dark out there and snowing harder – I can hardly see as far as the road.'

'Maybe your parents will get stuck in the snowstorm,' Jo worried.

'The jeep can get through almost any-thing,' Alex said. But she stood up and looked anxiously towards the door. 'Where are my juggling balls?'

The others watched silently as Alex rum-maged through her knapsack for her three soft, brightly-coloured balls. It was a sure sign that Alex was working out a problem

23

when she started to juggle. She flopped cross-legged in the armchair and began to toss one of the balls gently into the air.

Charlie bounced back to the couch. 'I don't know what you're all so worried about,' she said. 'The wolves can't get in, and as long as the food holds out, we'll be fine.'

She plopped down beside Louise. 'Remember our last sleepover? We were alone almost the whole night.'

'That was in Jo's nice safe basement!' Louise cried. 'Not stuck up on some mountain in the middle of a pack of howling wolves. Listen, it's starting again . . .'

The others stared at each other in alarm. It was a fearful sound. Louise dived under her sleeping bag.

'Tell us more about Jake,' Jo said at last, putting her arm around Louise's shaking shoulders. 'What happened when his parents went away to get the gold tested and left him with Digger?'

'It was the beginning of a bad time for Jake,' Alex said.

As Alex went on with her story, her words took them back to a winter six years before.

Up on the mountain, Jake put his guitar in its

case and shoved it under his bed in the loft. Digger was working in the mine, and had started both the gas-powered generators. It was useless to try to practise with that deadly machine noise thudding in his ears.

Jake dressed warmly and stepped out into the frosty air. The snow was too deep to go tramping through the woods on foot, so he reached for his snowshoes, leaning against the cabin wall. They were the 'bearpaw' type, each one shaped like a huge bear's footprint.

Jake had grown up in the north, and for him the time of deep snow was a time of freedom. The Native People knew this. They had designed snowshoes to walk far and fast on top of the snow.

Of course there was a trick to snowshoeing. Jake had learned how to swing each leg wide in front of the other in a steady rhythm.

He set off from the cabin and worked his way steadily up the ridge behind the mine, far from the thumping noise of the generators. He started to breathe more easily.

Somewhere, right under his feet, the tunnels and shafts of the Hook Mountain Mine twisted deep into the mountain's face. But up here the air was cold and clear and still.

He was exploring the ridge when he suddenly heard moaning, as if someone was in pain. Jake pushed through a screen of evergreen branches.

Something was caught in one of Digger's wolf traps! Jake heard the clank of metal chain. He glimpsed a white shape, thrashing and groaning in the snow.

'Help!' the struggling figure cried out.

Jake stood, frozen with astonishment. It was not a wolf, it was a girl. Luckily, Jake saw, she was wearing steel-toed boots and snowshoes. The teeth of the trap had snapped on the edge of one snowshoe, and the toe of her boot.

But Jake could tell it still hurt. The girl was trying to get her boot off, and get free.

For a second, he just stood there, speechless.

He had never seen such a beautiful person. She had long hair, almost white it was so blonde. Her face was golden brown, and her eyes were the colour of a clear blue sky.

She was wearing a long parka trimmed with fake fur, tied in at the waist.

'Can you help me?' she groaned again. 'I've got my other snowshoe twisted at a funny angle, and I can't get out of my boot.'

Jake finally snapped out of his trance and bent down to give her a hand. She looked up at him with her piercing blue eyes. 'You didn't set this trap, did you?' she blazed at him.

'No,' he said, but he had to tell the truth. 'It's my parents' partner, Digger, who is setting the traps. He's . . .'

The girl didn't let him finish. 'We know all about Digger,' she spat out his name.

Jake managed to get her foot out of her boot, and now he had to get the boot out of the trap. The spring on the leghold traps was strong, but he managed to pry the teeth apart, using all his strength.

'It was a good thing you were wearing these,' Jake said, looking at the deep scar in the boot leather.

'Thanks,' she said, reaching for the boot. 'I owe you one. What's your name?'

'Jake Kingston,' he told her. 'You don't owe me anything. I'm sorry about Digger . . .'

'Make him stop setting traps,' the girl said. She winced as she put her boot back on and stood up. 'Make him leave the wolves alone.'

Jake helped her dig her snowshoes out of the drift and strap them back on. He wanted to ask 'What's your name?', but somehow, he felt she would think he was being pushy. She must live around here, if she knew about Digger. The Bells would know who she was.

Without another word, the girl strode away with the wide, swinging stride of the snowshoer. Jake followed, but he was soon far behind and breathing hard.

He trailed her down the other side of the ridge, but she had disappeared into the thick pine forest. At last he gave up, and headed back to the mine. Tomorrow he would ask the Bells about her, and he would speak to Digger that night.

But Digger stayed late in the mine. The generators thudded on, and Jake could see the light burning in the entrance to the mine.

What was Digger doing? He hadn't spoken to Jake since his parents had left, had just looked at him with that twisted, mocking smile.

That night when Jake went out to the woodpile to get some firewood, he looked up and there was a shape, a grey shape, in the moonlight. Jake heard himself gasp. It was a huge grey wolf with blazing yellow eyes, almost close enough to touch, on the other side of the woodpile.

The wolf stood watching Jake, and its eyes glowed in the moonlight.

Something about those blank, golden eyes made Jake tremble to the centre of his being. He wanted to run and fight at the same time. The hair stood up on the back of his neck.

Without thinking, he reached for a heavy stick of firewood and raised his arm. The wolf paid no attention to the raised arm. All it did was stare at Jake with those fearsome, slanted eyes. Then it melted away into the snow with no sound.

Still trembling, Jake staggered back inside. Now his knees began to shake, and he sank down on the couch, realising how frightened he had been. One leap, and the wolf could have torn out his throat.

A moment later a sudden rifle shot shattered the night. Jake leapt to the door and flung it open. Digger was shooting at the wolf!

There was no sign of the wolf, or Digger. The echo of the gunshot was still bouncing off the face of the mountain, sounding again and again across the valley.

Jake had a flash memory of the girl on the mountain. 'Make Digger stop,' she had said. He had not kept his promise.

He went back inside the dim, quiet cabin,

and shut the door, feeling more alone than he had ever felt in his life.

The Bells heard the gunshots up on the mountain.

'What's happening up there?' Mrs Bell stood in the window with her hands on her hips. 'What can Jake's folks be thinking of, leaving him with that man!'

'Maybe it was life or death,' Mr Bell shrugged. 'Maybe if they don't get more money, they'll have to close the mine.'

'Life or death, indeed,' Mrs Bell snorted. 'Who has ever got any good out of that cold, rocky mountain? Even Willie Low went crazy and wandered off into the woods. Leave the place to the wolves and the bears, I say, and shut the mine down, for good.'

Mr Bell nodded. Prospectors were always coming into the store to show off their latest ore sample. But since Willie Low's big strike, no one had found enough gold to make them rich.

'Maybe the Kingstons found the mother lode this time,' Mr Bell sighed. He ruffled his thinning hair.

'Sure. And maybe the moon is made of apple pie,' Mrs Bell scolded. 'But I hope they do strike it rich, for Jake's sake.' She turned to her husband. 'Such a nice lad, with that big grin and those dark brown eyes.'

'And he's a worker,' Mr Bell nodded approvingly. 'He looks a bit stringy, but he's strong enough.'

'Well,' sighed Mrs Bell, 'I, for one, will be glad when the Kingstons get back to look after that boy.'

Five

The next morning Mr and Mrs Bell saw Digger drive through the Crossroads with a dead grey wolf in the back of his pickup.

They were relieved when Jake walked in a few minutes later. He had walked down the road to find out about the girl caught in Digger's trap.

'Do you know her?' he asked Mr Bell. 'She has long blonde hair, and wears a white coat, with fuzzy stuff around the bottom.'

'That must be Lucy,' Mr Bell said. 'Lucy Montgomery. She's a bit funny in the head, if you know what I mean.'

'And not a nice kind of girl for you to hang around with at all!' Mrs Bell bustled in from the back of the store, where she'd been listening to their conversation.

'Why?' Jake wanted to know. 'What's the matter with her?'

'Just goes her own way,' Mr Bell shook

his head. 'Doesn't care what people think.'

'Where does she live?' Jake was not going to give up that easily. He had to find Lucy and try to explain about the wolf that Digger had shot.

'Moves around a lot,' Mr Bell mumbled.

'Supposed to be living with the Turcottes now, isn't she, Mr B?' Mrs Bell said. 'But they can't control her. They never know where she is, day or night.'

Mrs Bell sniffed. 'She's lived with one or another family around here since her mother died. None of *them* could control her – just a wild thing!'

'She must be almost old enough to be on her own now,' Mr Bell put in. 'Sixteen, seventeen years old. But the dear Lord knows what will become of her. She won't stay in school, just runs wild.'

'She goes home to eat,' Mrs Bell nodded. 'That's about all.'

Jake thought of the girl he'd seen, snow-shoeing through the woods. Lucy looked like she could look after herself.

'What would she be doing up on the ridge above the mine?' Jake asked.

'She used to have a friend up there. A female prospector named Ruby LaFleur. Ruby had a shack at the back of the ridge,'

Mr Bell told him. 'Maybe she goes back up there for old times' sake.'

'Lucy spent a lot of time with Ruby – used to help her in the shack, bring her food . . .' Mrs Bell explained. 'Ruby was really too old to be living alone in the bush. It was Lucy who found her one day, freezing to death in bed, in her rubber boots, would you believe!'

'Lucy brought her down here to the store on a home-made toboggan,' Mr Bell jumped into the story. 'Ruby lost both her feet to gangrene, but she recovered. She still lives down the road a piece.'

Mrs Bell nodded. 'The whole shack was stacked to the rafters with old maps and papers. People figured it was a forest fire just waiting to happen, so they tore it down.'

Jake was only half listening. He was thinking about Lucy dragging her friend down the mountain on a toboggan. She didn't sound so crazy. He was about to say that to the Bells, when the door burst open and Digger strode in.

His face shone with dirt and sweat. 'Well? Is there any message?' Digger growled at Jake.

'Oh. Yeah,' Jake stammered. 'Did my parents get in touch with you?' he asked Mr Bell. 'Is there a message for me?'

The Bells had the only pay-phone in the area. Cellular phone networks didn't reach that far north, so they were a message centre for the whole Hook Mountain area.

'I suppose you didn't even ask them.' Digger looked disgusted.

'Now, easy. We were just getting around to that.' Mr Bell reached into a cubbyhole behind the counter. 'Jake had a special letter delivered last night.'

Digger reached for the letter, but Mr Bell snatched it away and handed it to Jake. 'It's addressed to the boy,' he said firmly, 'not to you, *Mr* Grimes.'

Jake tore open the envelope. He scanned the letter quickly and raised a face full of amazement.

'It's . . . good news,' he choked. 'The ore has very high gold content. They're sure they can raise more money . . .'

'When will they be back?' Mrs Bell shot in her question.

Jake read further. 'Not until next week. They have to get the lab reports, and see the bank on Monday . . .'

There was a silent moment in the store. The Bells looked at Digger, and Digger looked at the letter as if he'd like to rip it out of Jake's hand.

'They're my damn partners,' he growled. 'Why wouldn't they want me to get the message?'

'Maybe they just wanted *their son* to know first,' Mrs Bell sniffed.

Jake was still staring at the words on the page, as if he couldn't believe them.

At that moment, the door opened and Lucy stepped into the store.

She was still wearing the fur-trimmed parka and boots. Her eyes flew to Jake, and then Digger.

'You,' she said fiercely, pointing at him. 'You shot a wolf.'

Digger whipped round to face Lucy. He stared at her for a second, then shrugged. 'The animal was acting strange.' Digger's eyes went back to the paper in Jake's hand. 'He must have had rabies. I shot him, and took him down to the wildlife office to get him tested.'

'She,' Lucy said, her voice even lower. 'It wasn't a male wolf, it was a female. She had pups a few weeks ago.'

'Then what was she doing hanging around the mine?' Digger sneered. He still didn't look at Lucy.

'She was weak with hunger,' Lucy said. 'She was looking for food.' She glared at

Digger. 'You'll be sorry if you don't stop trapping wolves, and shooting them.'

'Says who?' Digger whirled round. 'I don't like wolves. They're dangerous animals. Jake, get in the truck. We don't have time to stand around listening to this. We've got work to do!'

Jake glanced at Lucy. He felt terrible about the wolf Digger shot. He felt ashamed just being there with Digger.

'I'll walk back up to the mine,' he finally said. Now it was too late to explain.

'Now, that's a stupid waste of time, isn't it? We've got work to do!' Digger grabbed Jake by the arm. 'Come on, get in the truck.'

Jake jerked away from Digger's grip. He calmly folded the letter from his parents and stuck it in his pocket. He pulled on his work gloves and zipped his parka. 'I'll see you up at the mine,' he said. 'I'm walking.'

Digger banged out into the road, slamming the door behind him.

'Good riddance to bad rubbish,' Mrs Bell said.

Jake just nodded. He watched Digger drive off in the pickup, grinding his gears and throwing up a spray of snow from under the tyres.

'I'll be in tomorrow,' he told the Bells. 'I'm waiting for a music book to come in the mail.' He looked at Lucy. 'Goodbye,' he said. 'I'll see you.'

Lucy gave a quick shake of her long blonde hair. Jake turned and walked out of the store. They watched him walk slowly up in the direction of the mine.

Mrs Bell shook her head.

'Did you see the greed on that man's face, when Jake was reading the news about the gold?' she said. 'His eyes were glittering, that's what they were.'

Alex reached for the chunk of ore in the metal box. 'I wonder how Jake felt when he read the good news about the gold?' she said. As she turned the rock in the fire's glow, the others could see the gold pick up the light.

'Look in the diary,' Jo suggested.

Alex found the place where she'd stopped reading. 'OK, here's something . . .' she bent over the cramped writing, holding the book close to the candle. 'The writing's even worse than usual. Hey! Listen to this!'

Saturday, Feb. 4
The wolves have been howling and

Digger has been drinking ever since he shot the grey wolf. He says the werewolf will be out to get him for sure, now. He hears it howling his name, and catches glimpses of a big white wolf lurking around the mine. He keeps his gun beside him all the time.

I hate the look on his face. It's even meaner than usual. He wants me to go down in the mine with him tonight – to check the new seam of gold. I don't want to go, but he keeps calling me a sissy. I don't know how much longer I can stand this . . .

Alex's voice trailed off. 'It's too hard to read!' she exclaimed. She looked around the cabin, which was now pitch-black except for the pool of light around the stove. 'I wish my mum and dad would get back with the lantern fuel.'

Alex stood up and went to the woodbox for more wood. 'Listen to the wind, whistling through the cracks in the wall. What's happening out there?' she cried, suddenly alarmed.

Six

'You can't stop reading now!' Jo cried. 'What's happening to Jake?'

Alex dropped the wood back in the box with a thud. 'I'm going to take a look outside,' she told them, reaching for the door handle.

'Oh, please don't open the door,' Louise cried.

'For heaven's sake, Louise, what do you think is going to rush in? A ravening wolf? A frozen prospector in her rubber boots?' Alex jerked at the heavy cabin door.

A blast of snow and wind nearly flung her backwards to the floor. The wind howled through the open door, whirling snow to the furthest reaches of the cabin, wrapping them in its icy fury.

'Shut that door!' Charlie shouted, springing up to help Alex. Together, leaning against it, they managed to bang the door shut and latch it.

The four friends stared at each other.

'Well,' Charlie gulped. 'Now we know what rushed in – an entire snowstorm!'

'It's a real blizzard,' Alex gasped. 'I don't think even the jeep can get through that!'

'How can we find out? There's no phone in this place!' Charlie looked around the dark cabin. 'No telephone, no TV, no radio. We're totally cut off.'

'What about your portable CD player?' Jo asked Alex suddenly. 'Doesn't it have a radio?'

Charlie made a dive for it. 'Smart thinking, Jo! Maybe they'll have a weather forecast, or news.' She flipped her dark hair behind her ears and fiddled with the buttons on the radio.

'Nothing . . . nothing . . . nothing . . .' Charlie threw up her arms in despair. 'We *are* at the end of the world up here!'

All at once there was the crackle of static, then a clear voice:

'. . . a freak blizzard has dumped over 45 centimetres of snow in this mountain region in the past hour. Police and highway crews are reporting the roads in the Smith Peak, Ply Valley and Hook Mountain area are completely blocked. High winds and blowing and drifting snow have reduced visibility to zero. Police are warning motorists to stay off the highways . . .'

The voice blurred out.

Jo and Alex, Charlie and Louise stared at each other in the flickering candlelight.

'I guess that means we're stuck here by ourselves, for a while,' Jo finally gulped.

'I hope Mum and Dad aren't stuck somewhere in a snowdrift,' Alex said anxiously.

'Don't worry,' Charlie had recovered her good spirits now that the radio worked. 'I'm sure your dad has enough survival gear packed into that jeep for an arctic expedition. And we've still got lots of food – which is the main thing.' Charlie ripped open a bag of chips and passed them around.

'How can you just keep eating, with a blizzard blowing out there?' Louise gasped.

'We have to keep calm,' Charlie shrugged.

Jo gave Louise a quick hug. 'Why don't you tell us more about Jake?' she asked Alex. 'What happened to him?'

Alex flopped back in her armchair, dusting the snow out of her mop of curls. 'I guess it would help keep our mind off things if I keep telling the story.' She leaned forward to poke at the logs with a steel poker, sending up a shower of sparks.

'Six years ago,' she said, 'in this very place, Jake was in even worse trouble than we are.'

Alex cleared her throat and began to speak in her normal, no-nonsense voice.

You remember that Digger wanted Jake to go down in the mine with him. You can't see the entrance to the mine now – it's buried in snow – but there's a big steel door cut in the rock, near the gate. That's how you get in.

Digger had his rifle cocked and ready as he and Jake stepped out of the cabin. He motioned Jake to walk ahead. 'Those wolves,' he muttered. 'They're like ghosts. They just come out of nowhere. Can't you feel them, watching us?'

Jake hated to admit it, but he couldn't help remembering how suddenly, how *silently*, the grey wolf had appeared the night before at the woodpile – the horrible jolt in the pit of his stomach when he looked up and saw the wolf staring at him.

He and Digger crossed the snowy, moon-lit clearing. Jake wrenched open the metal mine door and stepped into the blackness inside.

Behind him, Digger flipped the generator switch and the motor thudded into life, filling the cave-like entrance with noise. At the same time, lights flickered on and the sound of two electric pumps started up. One of them pumped out the water that seeped into the tunnels. The other sent fresh air hissing into the deep underground spaces.

'That's more like it, eh, sissy?' Digger sneered. 'You don't like the dark, dirty mine much, do you? Dark as the dungeon, they say, down in the mine.'

'Let's just hurry up,' Jake said. 'Do whatever you have to do in here—'

'Oh, I will, I will,' Digger laughed nastily. 'You just walk ahead, down the main tunnel. Let's go see the pretty gold that Digger found.'

The guy was really drunk, Jake thought. He wished he hadn't come. It was damp and chill in the tunnel, and their boots crunched on loose rock making echoes even louder than the generator noise.

Digger had to yell his directions. 'Down this ladder,' he bellowed, at last.

'I didn't think the new seam was down here,' Jake shouted back. By now they were a long way from the entrance, in an unused part of the mine.

'I should know,' Digger shouted in Jake's ear. Jake jumped at hearing the voice so close, and found the rifle pointed at his belt buckle. 'I'm the one who found it.'

Jake's insides twisted with fear.

'Down there!' Digger said. It was an order, backed up by a swing of the rifle. Digger's pale sweaty face gleamed in the light of the naked bulbs strung from the roof of the tunnel.

Jake looked down the narrow opening leading into the darkness below. It had rusty iron rungs set into a rock shaft which was just wide enough for one miner to descend at a time.

Jake started down. When he looked up, Digger's drunken leer seemed to fill the opening above. 'I'll wait here until you're all the way down,' Digger said. 'Just keep going.'

Jake's hands were clammy on the cold iron rungs. His heart raced. At last, Jake felt his feet touch ground at the next level.

'There's no light down here,' he called up, hearing his voice crack.

'Well, we'll have to fix that, won't we,'

Digger's voice echoed down the shaft. 'How about a nice little burst of light.'

Jake saw a fizz of sparkling fire near the top of the shaft. It took a few seconds to register in his terrified brain that it was a burning fuse in Digger's hand, and by then Digger was laughing.

'You'd better run, sissy boy,' Digger cackled. 'I've lit the fuse, attached to a nice little dynamite charge that should land just there, by your feet.'

'What are you doing?' Jake screamed.

'The gold is mine,' Digger roared. His voice echoed 'Mine – mine – mine' up and down the tunnel. 'You fancy geologists didn't find it – the *Digger* found it. You're going to have an accident. And then Mummy and Daddy aren't going to be around much longer either. And then, old buddy Digger's going to be the only partner left to get rich.'

'You're crazy!' Jake screamed, as the burning fuse and a dark bundle came hurtling down the shaft.

There was no time to do anything but run for his life down the pitch-black tunnel before the dynamite exploded.

The Bells got worried when Jake didn't show

up at the store all the next day. That was a Saturday, and Jake's parents weren't due back until at least Monday.

'It's almost four o'clock. I think we should try to call the Kingstons,' Mrs Bell said.

'It's none of our business, Mrs B.' Mr Bell shook his head.

'And I suppose it's none of our business if that boy comes to harm?' Mrs Bell picked up the telephone.

'We don't have any idea where his folks are staying,' Mr Bell groaned, 'and it's long-distance to the city.'

Mrs Bell just ignored him, and started calling information for hotel numbers.

'Hold it,' Mr Bell hissed, after the fifth call. 'Digger is out there. He wants something in the garage.'

Mr Bell hunched into his parka and hurried outside. 'What can I do for you today?' he said, eyeing Digger carefully.

Digger hunched the shoulders of his green parka. 'Gas for the truck. I'll take some more dynamite, too, and a bottle of rum from the store,' he said.

Mr Bell pretended to laugh. 'Well, now. Rum and dynamite. That could be a dangerous mixture.'

'Mind your own business,' Digger snarled.

47

'One more remark like that,' Mr Bell growled back, 'and you can take *your* business elsewhere!'

Digger backed down. There was nowhere else to buy supplies and gas, and he knew it. He bought a case of dynamite and his bottle of rum, and got back in the truck.

'You and Jake working hard up there?' Mr Bell asked, as Digger dug the money out of his pocket.

'I'm keeping him busy,' Digger sneered. 'That sissy boy's got to learn the meaning of hard work.' He laughed, as if at a private joke, then slammed the truck door and roared away up the mountain.

Mr Bell went back in the store, and hung his parka on the hook inside the door.

'Well?' Mrs Bell said.

'Keep phoning,' Mr Bell told her. 'I don't like the look, the sound, or the smell of that man.'

Seven

When Jake woke up, cramped and hurting, it took a few minutes to remember what had happened. It was pitch-black in the mine tunnel and the smell of dynamite poisoned the air. It was the smell that suddenly brought it all back – running in the dark – the concussion of the explosion – the blast that had thrown him head-first down the tunnel.

He touched his aching head. There was a lump the size of a tangerine on his forehead. He was lucky to be alive.

Or was he?

He felt his way up the dark tunnel to a solid wall of rock and debris. He tore at the rock until his fingers bled. There was no way to break through. Digger, with his precision skill with dynamite, had sealed the tunnel, cutting off the ladder to the upper level.

Jake crouched in the blackness. It was so

quiet he could hear the sound of his own ragged breath, the steady drip, drip, drip of water. Over his head he could sense the weight of thousands of tons of rock. He was caught like an animal in a trap. At least the generator was turned off. The constant throbbing would have made his headache worse.

And then Jake realised the full horror of his situation. With no electricity from the generator, the pump wouldn't work. This tunnel would soon fill up with water.

What a stupid jerk he had been to follow Digger into the mine! Digger had spent his life looking for the big strike. Now that he had found gold, he was ready to kill rather than share it. Kill Jake, kill his partners.

'I have to think,' Jake told himself. He slumped back against the rocky wall of the tunnel, his head in his hands. He could picture his trusting parents walking into Digger's trap.

Moments later, he heard a sound that made him lift his head. Jake felt his ears tingle, the hair rise on the back of his neck. What was it? Every tiny sound was magnified in the darkness.

Jake's heart thudded in his chest.

It was not dripping. It was more like

footsteps, but softer. He could hear little rocks skittering away.

Now he smelled a sour, animal smell. He could hear the animal sniff the air. It stopped moving forward, and sniffed again. Jake pressed his body into a crack in the rock until he could not retreat any further, but the sniffing came closer, and closer.

Suddenly, he felt something wet touch his face.

Something was licking his face! At any second he expected to feel the teeth . . .

All at once, the licking, sniffing snout was gone. Jake could tell by the sounds that the animal had taken a few steps away. He forced himself to suck in a deep breath. He must not display fear in the darkness.

Because now he could smell it, feel it, coming back.

What did it want?

Jake's mind was starting to work. How had the animal got in here? Maybe it had been sealed in the tunnel when Digger set off the dynamite blast. Or maybe it knew another way out.

It was already getting wet and cold underneath him. He had two choices – to stay and drown, or follow the creature.

Jake beat back his panic. He rose slowly

51

to his feet. His head was spinning, but he went stumbling forward, following the soft splashing footsteps in the flooded tunnel. Sometimes, the animal was far ahead. Other times it seemed almost underfoot.

As they went on, Jake could feel the tunnel getting lower. Moments later, he struck his head on a spur of rock. He knew he would have to get down on all fours.

He crawled on his hands and knees for hours, it seemed. At last, far ahead, Jake saw a glimmer of light. He crawled forward eagerly – the tunnel was now so low he had to keep his head down. When he glanced up, to see the light again, Jake's heart almost stopped.

The animal was blocking the tunnel, facing him. It had wolf's eyes, blank golden discs, slanted and horrible. Jake forced himself to look away, to turn his head to one side. There was a long moment of silence, and then the wolf turned and padded on.

Now, the tunnel turned sharply upwards. It became even narrower. Loose dirt cascaded down around Jake, choking him.

There was something soft and squirmy in the space ahead, making small whimpering noises. Cold noses nuzzled his face. Jake realised where he was – in the middle of a litter of wolf cubs, crying for their mother. The mother wolf was not coming back to the den. She was the grey wolf Digger had shot. The wolf he had followed must be another member of the pack.

Careful not to crush the cubs, Jake wriggled on his belly out of the den and into the even tighter entrance tunnel. The frozen earth pressed tight around his body in an icy grip.

Terror gripped him. What if he got stuck here, so close to freedom? His shoulders were much wider than a wolf's body. Desperately, he clawed at the dirt with his bare hands.

And then a hand fastened around his wrist. A strong arm pulled him, gasping, towards the glimmer of light ahead.

Suddenly he was out, lying in the snow, sucking in huge lungfuls of fresh, cold air. His vision was blurred, but he thought he saw a girl in a white coat, with blonde hair shining in the moonlight, bending over him.

'Lucy!' Jake gave one astonished cry, and blacked out completely.

A few minutes later he woke to find Lucy pressing fresh snow against his forehead. He sat up, still groggy. 'Where am I?' he stammered.

'Be quiet . . . hurry!' Lucy said. 'We are still near the mine.' She helped Jake strap snowshoes on his feet and stumble through the woods, leaning on her shoulder.

They climbed a narrow, winding trail up the ridge. The trail led into the pine forest on the other side. In the heart of the dense forest was a small shack. It had no windows, and no real door, just a canvas flap to keep out the wind and snow.

But inside there was a fire in a rusted barrel stove, and rough wool blankets. Lucy settled Jake on the blankets. She made sure the stove was blazing hard, and showed Jake where the firewood was stacked in the corner.

'You'll be all right, here,' Lucy murmured.

'I'll be fine,' Jake nodded. He was so happy to be alive, so happy to be there with Lucy that he didn't care about the bump on his head, the cold, the hard bed.

'I have to go now,' Lucy said. 'I have to cover our trail from the mine.' She fixed him with her fierce blue eyes. 'Listen to me, Jake. You must stay here. Don't go making tracks in the snow. Digger tried to kill you, but you'll be safe as long as he thinks you're down in that mine.'

'What is this place?' Jake gasped.

54

'It's my place,' Lucy said. 'I built it.'
She straightened up. 'I'll be back tomorrow. Wait for me.' She glanced quickly around the little shack, and then disappeared through the canvas flap.

'Amazing!' Charlie exclaimed. 'The wolves must have used the old mine tunnels as part of their den.'
'I wonder what Lucy was doing there?' Jo said.
'She was the wolves' friend,' Charlie reminded them.
'I don't know . . .' Louise said. 'Maybe that poor girl we heard about on the radio, the one that was killed by wolves – maybe she thought the wolves were her friends – until they attacked her!' Louise shuddered.

Eight

'You see what happens when parents leave kids alone?' Louise cried. 'Jake was almost killed!'

'You said the Kingstons *had* a son,' Jo turned to Alex. 'Did Digger find him at Lucy's shack? Is that why they shut down the mine, because Jake died?'

Alex just picked up her juggling balls again and shook her head. 'Why don't you let me tell the story,' she said.

Alex stared into the dancing flames of the wood stove. Her voice held them fascinated as she began to tell Jake's story again.

The Bells opened their store at noon on Sunday in the winter. This Sunday was dark and dreary, with low clouds hanging over the mountain.

At twelve o'clock Mr Bell unlocked the

front door. Mrs Bell wiped the lids of the candy jars on the counter. 'We never got through to Jake's parents. Maybe you should take a drive up to the mine, and see if the boy is all right,' Mrs Bell fussed.

'And what good would that do, Mrs B? Digger Grimes would throw me out as soon as I drove through the gate. Besides, you know my policy . . .'

'Of course I know it. Don't get mixed up with the mining people. Just take their money and keep their secrets,' Mrs Bell sighed. 'But there's a fifteen-year-old boy, all alone up there with a crazy man. Can't you think of some excuse to go up there?'

At that moment the door slammed open and Digger himself stumbled in. He was weaving from side to side. He propped himself against the counter and gazed at the Bells with bloodshot eyes.

'Humph!' sniffed Mrs B. 'Drinking, this time of day, and on a Sunday!'

'Mind your own business,' Digger snarled. 'It's a working day for me. Yes, sir, I've got lots of work to do.'

He pointed to the back of the store, where the Bells kept hardware, and prospecting supplies. 'More dynamite,' he growled. 'I need lots more.'

Mr Bell raised one eyebrow, but said nothing. 'Anything else for you today?' he asked.

'Some tape fuses and a roll of wire,' Digger growled. 'And make it fast, will you?'

A few minutes later he was loading the dynamite on the truck and spinning his wheels as he drove away.

'Well?' Mrs Bell stood with her hands on her plump hips.

'It's a funny thing, needing all that dynamite,' Mr Bell shook his head. 'But I may have to drive up there, after all. It seems Mr Digger Grimes forgot his fuses . . .' Mr Bell pulled a small bag out from under the counter.

'Mr Bell, you're a sneaky one,' Mrs Bell smiled.

Late Sunday afternoon, Lucy came back to the shelter in the pines.

Jake was gathering wood, snapping off dead branches low on the trunks of the balsams. Lucy just appeared beside him, without warning, walking silently over the snow on her snowshoes. She had a bulging knapsack on her back.

'I brought you some food, and another blanket,' she smiled. Her smile was wide and turned up at the corners.

'Thank you,' Jake said, staring at her. 'I appreciate all you're doing for me, but I can't stay here. I have to find out what Digger is doing down at the mine. I know he's making some kind of trap for my parents.'

Lucy shook her head. 'If you snowshoe down there, Digger will be able to track you right back to this shack,' she said. 'Anyway, I have some news. I'll tell you while I make us some tea.'

Lucy led the way into the shelter. She slipped off her knapsack, and opened it. In the dim light of the little hut, Jake could see her eyes glowing as she flipped back her long silver-blonde hair. She was beautiful. She brought out a small box of tea. Her nose twitched as she held it to her nose and sniffed.

'This will warm you up. I got it at the Crossroads Store . . .' she began.

'Thank you. I'll pay you back,' Jake stammered. He hated to depend on Lucy, but the sight of food reminded him he hadn't eaten all day.

'Don't worry about it.' She waved her hand. 'I heard something while I was in the store. The Bells said Digger had been in a few minutes earlier. He was drunk and buying more dynamite.'

Jake stood up quickly and banged his head on the roof. Lucy had built the shack just high enough for herself, but she was shorter than Jake. 'You see why I have to go down there?' he cried out. 'He's building some kind of booby trap for my parents . . .'

'Settle down.' Lucy's eyes flashed a warning. 'They won't be back until tomorrow. Anyway, the Bells are worried about you. They've been trying to reach your mum and dad in the city. I didn't tell them I'd seen you – they might tell Digger.

'But don't worry,' Lucy went on. 'I'll find a way to stop Digger before your parents get to the mine tomorrow . . . You stay here, and stay safe.'

She pawed through a pile of stuff behind the stove and brought out an old metal pot. 'This is what we need to boil water for the tea.'

'But I feel so helpless,' Jake fumed. 'I've been hanging around here all day. I feel like I have to do something!'

'Then go out and fill this with snow,' Lucy handed Jake the pot. 'It takes a lot of melted snow to make a pot of water.'

Jake obediently went outside to pack the pot full of fresh snow. 'Thank you for letting me stay in your place,' he said shyly, coming through the flap into the warmth of the little hut. 'Where did you get the materials to build it?'

'From my friend Ruby LaFleur's cabin,' Lucy explained. 'When they tore it down I saved the stove and the lumber and tin roof, and made my own place. Sometimes, I need to get away from the foster home where I'm living.'

'You did a terrific job,' Jake shook his head. 'If you weren't looking for it, you'd pass right by this clump of balsam without knowing the shack was here.'

Lucy flushed with pleasure. 'It's the same in the summer when the leaves hide the roof,' she said. 'The only time someone might spot it is in the spring and autumn.' She took the pot of snow and set it on the stove. It hissed as the snow melted on the hot metal.

She threw a handful of tea in the pot on the stove, and rummaged in her pack for some bread and cheese. 'Have some of this,' she said. 'You must be starving.'

The tea and food made Jake feel much stronger. He found himself staring at Lucy. She looked so beautiful with the rays of the setting sun coming through chinks in the wall of the shack.

'Can I ask you s-something?' Jake stammered.

Lucy raised her remarkable blue eyes to him.

'How did you come to be at the wolf's den, just when I needed you?'

Lucy smiled her strange, turned-up grin. 'You were lucky,' she said. 'When I heard the dynamite explosion at the mine, I thought I'd better come up and check on the wolf cubs. I couldn't believe my eyes when I peered in and saw you stuck in the entrance!'

Jake felt a pang of guilt for the motherless cubs. 'How are they doing?' he asked.

Lucy smiled again. 'They're lucky, too. They're eight weeks old – big enough to survive without their mother. The other pack members will bring them food, and teach them how to get along in the world.'

'Like foster parents,' Jake said.

Lucy's smile vanished. '*Not* like foster parents!' she said. 'More like uncles and aunts – like family.' There was a note of both anger and sadness in her voice.

'How can you trust the wolves?' Jake asked. 'I mean, they're still wild animals, savage killers.'

Now Lucy was really angry. 'That's a lie!'

she cried, her eyes gleaming. 'Wolves kill to eat. They only kill the wounded, and the weak. If you ask me, the only savage killers in these mountains are people. Men like Digger Grimes!'

She gathered up her belongings, and stuffed them in her knapsack. 'I have to go,' she said coldly. 'There's enough food here to last until your parents get back, if you're careful.'

She moved towards the door. 'Remember, Digger thinks you're dead, or dying in the mine. Stay here. Let me deal with Digger.'

'I can't do that!' Jake tried to stand up and banged his head again. 'These are my parents we're talking about! At least tell the Bells what's happening, and get the police.'

Lucy laughed scornfully. 'The Bells wouldn't believe anything I told them. And the same goes for the police. I'm known around here as a no-good teenage runaway, in case you hadn't heard.'

Jake reached out his arm to touch her, but Lucy flinched away. 'I . . . I think you're amazing,' he told her.

Lucy gave him an odd look. 'Thank you,' she said. 'I'm not sure what side you're on, but I think I can trust you. I like your music.' And then she was gone.

Jake sat back on the blankets, numb with surprise. How did Lucy know about his music?

SNAP! A sudden loud crack made Alex jump.

'What was that?' Louise clutched the sleeping bag tight around her throat.

'I don't know . . .' Alex got up slowly, stretching her long legs, and tiptoeing across the cabin floor. 'It came from up there . . .' She pointed up at the loft.

Charlie followed her. They peered up into the darkness at the top of the ladder.

'There's something up there,' Charlie whispered. 'I can hear noises.'

'But what was that loud snapping sound?' Jo asked. 'It sounded almost like a gunshot.'

'Get me the candle,' Alex said in a low voice.

Charlie tiptoed back to the stove and brought her the candle in its brass candle-holder.

'I'll hold it while you climb the ladder,' she whispered. 'Then you can reach down and grab it, and I'll climb up behind you.'

'What if there's someone hiding up there?' Louise stammered. 'Please, don't go.'

Nine

'C'mon, Louise,' Jo said, peeling the sleeping bag off her friend and pulling her up by the hand. 'Let's go and check out the loft. We're all in this together.'

They climbed the ladder's narrow rungs, and crouched on the floor beside Alex and Charlie.

They waited, listening.

Beneath the sound of the howling wind, they heard the scurry of many feet.

'Sounds like little animals!' Jo cried.

Alex held up the candle and peered around the shadowy loft. 'If it's just little animals,' she said, 'what made that loud bang?'

'Give me the candle,' Charlie said. 'Let me look.' She shone the light around the sagging old beds and dressers in the loft.

'I think . . . maybe under here . . .' Charlie stuck her arm under the bed.

'OW! OH! HELP!' she suddenly screamed. 'My hand! It ate my hand!'

She held up her arm with an empty sweater cuff.

Louise shrieked and lunged backwards.

'Careful,' Jo shouted. 'You'll fall down the ladder-hole.' She reached out to steady her friend.

'Sorry, Louise, just kidding.' Charlie pulled her hand back out of her sleeve, and wiggled her fingers. 'There's nothing under the bed except this . . .' She held up a mousetrap. 'There's your loud noise. The trap snapped, that's all.'

'Charlie!' Alex cried. 'You shouldn't *do* things like that.'

'Sorry,' Charlie giggled. 'You were all so jumpy, I couldn't resist.'

'A mousetrap!' Jo made a face. 'Ugh. Is there a dead mouse, too?'

'Nope,' Charlie shone the light under the bedspread. 'It looks like the mouse made a clean getaway.' She was still chuckling.

'So, where's the mouse now?' Alex reached for the candle. She shone the candle around the floor.

'Probably hiding right above your head in the rafters,' Charlie laughed.

'I hope it *does* chew your hand off, in your

sleep,' Louise scolded as they clambered back down the ladder. 'That was a rotten trick!'

'I couldn't believe you'd really fall for it,' Charlie laughed. 'The old hand-cut-off-at-the-cuff. It's the oldest trick in the book.'

'If you're finished clowning around, let Alex get back to telling us what happened to Jake and Lucy,' Jo said.

'Wait! I'm going to get some cereal,' Charlie said, making another dive at the food box. 'That mouse-hunting gave me an appetite.'

She found cereal and a carton of milk in the box. Alex showed them where to find bowls and spoons in the kitchen cupboards.

The four huddled back under their sleeping bags with their bowls of cereal.

As the fire burned lower, the circle of warmth around it shrank. Outside the circle, draughts whistled along the floor and chilled the corners of the cabin. They snuggled close to the warmth of the stove, to listen.

Alex picked up her juggling balls again. They caught the firelight as she tossed them one by one into the air. She began to speak.

Sunday night, Jake was alone in the shack. There was nothing to do but feed sticks into the fire in the stove, and wait.

But Jake's mind was racing. How had he let Lucy talk him into doing nothing, while she tackled Digger? This was crazy!

'They're *my* parents!' He broke off a stick and tossed it to the flames.

'It's *our* gold he's trying to steal.' Another stick sailed into the fire.

'*I'm* the one Digger tried to kill.' He cracked another stick.

'And she's a *girl*. I can't let her fight my battles.'

This last argument brought Jake surging to his feet. 'Ouch!' Banging his head was the final straw. He pulled aside the canvas curtain and looked out.

It was a calm night, with the moon almost full. The moonlight on white snow was so bright Jake could see the shadows of the birch trunks, like black bars across the smooth white surface. Behind bars was where Digger belonged. It was time to go back to the mine, and stop Digger.

Lucy was right about one thing, he thought. He had the element of surprise on his side. But Jake knew it would be risky. Once Digger realised he had escaped from the mine, he would be more desperate than ever to kill him.

Jake crawled through the low door, found

his snowshoes leaning against the wall beside the door, and strapped them on.

Snowshoeing through deep powder snow in the moonlight was like walking on a cloud. Jake strode along the top of the ridge until he was right above the cabin and the mine.

The generator was running again, filling the night with its noise. There were lights in the cabin windows, and another dim light in the entrance to the mine.

'I have to find a way to get down there,' Jake thought out loud, 'without leaving a trail back to Lucy's shack.' How could he get to the mine without leaving a wide, clear snowshoe trail?

Where Jake was standing, the ridge was a sheer cliff, as high as a house. The regular trail wound down a gentler slope of the ridge, further on. But what if he jumped from here, straight down? Digger would never connect that trail to one that began so high above it. No one would be crazy enough to jump off a ten-metre cliff.

As a kid, Jake had jumped off shed roofs into deep snow, for fun. It was all right if you were lucky and didn't hit something solid under the surface of the snow.

Jake took off his snowshoes, and pitched them over the edge. They sank out of sight in the snow. Then he waded to the edge of the rock cliff, took a deep breath, and launched himself into space, arms spread wide.

Down he plummeted, through the moonlight, soundlessly, like a snowy owl dropping on its prey.

Whoosh! The impact almost knocked the wind out of him. He was enveloped in snow to his armpits. Jake waited a second for the world to stop spinning and then started digging for his snowshoes and trying to wriggle himself free of the snow.

At that moment the lights of a truck, approaching the mine gate, came swinging through the trees. His parents! Jake thought in a panic – he must hurry. They must not go into the mine! There was no time to find the snowshoes.

Jake plunged forward through the deep snow. He could see Digger come out of the mine entrance and stand silhouetted against the lights of the truck. If he could just get there before his parents walked into Digger's trap!

Mr Bell's headlights lit up the Hook Mountain Mine gate. The bag of fuses was on the seat beside him. He pulled up at the gate and honked three times.

Three honks was a friendly signal in this part of the world. It meant you weren't a stranger. A good idea to let Digger know that, Mr Bell thought – especially since Digger had a rifle.

Digger came out of the mine entrance, blinking at the headlights. He walked over to the truck window, his rifle in the crook of his arm.

'What do you want, Bell?' he growled.

'I thought you might need your fuses,' Mr Bell said, holding up the bag. 'You left them behind today.'

Digger's nasty smile returned to his face. 'Nice of you to bring them.' Digger spat in the snow. 'It turned out we already had some. Too bad you wasted a trip.' He laughed nastily.

'You and Jake working hard?' Mr Bell asked.

'Hard enough,' Digger said. 'I'll get back to it, if you get your truck out of my way.'

Mr Bell was desperate. 'I . . . I got another message for Jake,' he said.

'Tell me,' Digger said. 'I'll give it to him.'

'Well, I'd sort of like to deliver it to Jake personally,' Mr Bell said. 'It's a personal message.'

'Then it will have to wait.' Digger gave a nasty grin. 'The kid's asleep. I guess he had kind of a hard day.'

71

Ten

Plunging through the snow towards the mine, Jake heard the three blasts of the truck horn. He froze, listening. That was not their truck – the horn sounded too high and tinny. But it might be someone else who could help him. Jake plunged forward again.

Too late! He could see the truck start to back up and turn to go down the mountain again. It was no use shouting for help. His call would be drowned by the noise of the truck motor and the chug of the generator.

Now he was out in the open. At any instant, Digger would turn round and spot him. But he might have a few seconds while Digger's eyes were blinded by the truck headlights. Jake raced forward and dived through the open door in the rock, into the mine entrance.

His eyes darted around the dimly-lit entrance. A short distance down the main tunnel, Jake saw a long dangling fuse. He followed it to a bundle of dynamite, wired to the ceiling. Digger was building the trap for his parents all right, like a spider spinning a deadly web.

Jake knew at any moment Digger would be back to finish the job. He yanked the wires loose from the rock ceiling and shoved the bundle of dynamite inside his coat.

He could hear Digger coming back. He had to get out of there.

Digger's footsteps crunched towards him. Jake pressed himself into the shadows of the tunnel and held his breath.

Digger paused in the opening to the tunnel. His eyes travelled up, to the dynamite that wasn't there, to the ripped wire, and down, until his eyes met Jake's.

For a moment, Jake saw shock and horror on Digger's face. He thinks I'm a ghost! Jake realised – the guy he buried at the bottom of the shaft. But before he could act, Digger's eyes narrowed to pinpoints of meanness. He swung his rifle up and pointed it at Jake.

'It looks like I didn't quite finish what I started yesterday,' Digger shook his head. He was still confused, and probably drunk, Jake thought.

'You keep coming back, trying to get my gold!' Digger's voice rose to an evil screech.

'This time, I'll make sure you don't come back! Move! Back up, out of the mine!'

Jake slowly retreated, his mind racing, his eyes fixed on the barrel of the rifle pointed at his chest.

'Keep going,' Digger said, when they were outside. 'Back up, into the snow.'

Jake felt every sense in his body tingling with terror. He could feel the cold on his cheeks. He could hear the swoosh of his boots in the powdery snow as he shuffled backwards, and taste the fear in his mouth. He could see the moonlight, glancing off the metal of the rifle barrel.

And then he saw a white shape emerging out of the snow behind Digger – a huge white wolf like a ghost with glowing eyes flying through the air.

There was a THUMP! as the white wolf collided with Digger's body. There was a shout of terror and the crack of a rifle going off, all at the same time.

Then a howl of pain, and the zigzag run of a wounded wolf.

Digger, bellowing with rage, was fumbling through the deep snow for his rifle. In the wolf's attack, it had flown out of his hands.

Jake turned and ran, plunging through the drifts, back towards the trees. It was

74

hopeless to make any speed in the thigh-deep snow, but it was his only chance.

He was following a dark trail of blood across the moonlit snow. The white wolf must be badly wounded.

Behind him he could hear Digger cursing, searching for his rifle.

All at once, he heard a wild burst of snarls, growls and terrified shouts. Jake glanced behind him.

The sight made him fall to his knees in astonishment. A circle of seven more wolves had surrounded Digger. They were not attacking, but they would not let him pick up his rifle. Every time he reached down, one of them, snapping and growling, would dash forward.

Slowly, the circle tightened, moving Digger towards the cabin and away from his gun.

Jake didn't stay to see any more. He plunged forward in the deep snow.

At the top of the ridge, Jake almost fell over the body of the white wolf. For a second, he stood looking down at the still bundle of silvery fur in the moonlight, feeling waves of pity and sorrow sweep over him. He could see that the wolf's right foreleg was covered in blood.

Then, he caught a slight movement out of the corner of his eye. Just a tiny flick of a tail. He saw the white fur on the wolf's chest lift and fall in a long sigh. It was still breathing!

Jake took a step back, feeling the fear of wolves rise in him again. For a moment, he thought of leaving the wolf there. It would be almost impossible to carry such a heavy load through the deep snow, with no snowshoes. Maybe the wolf would die anyway. Maybe it would attack him if he tried to move it.

But the wolf had saved his life. Jake suddenly felt ashamed. He bent low, and whispered urgently to the wolf. 'I'm going to lift you up. Don't be afraid.'

He bent closer, touched the wolf's shoulder. With a sudden snarl, the wolf snapped its head around and clamped its long white fangs on Jake's arm. With a shout of terror, Jake leapt to his feet, shaking his arm hard.

The wolf's jaws loosened, and Jake pulled his arm free. The huge white beast was standing now, swaying a little, its head down. The moonlight reflected off its glowing, slanted eyes. Jake could not move. He had seen those eyes before – in the tunnel, in the wolf's den!

The wolf turned, gave him one more look with its terrible blank eyes, and disappeared like a shadow in the trees.

Shaking, pumped with fear, Jake plunged on through the snow. Once or twice, he thought he saw grey shadows slipping in and out of the trees beside him, and that drove him forward. He reached Lucy's shack at last, threw himself inside and collapsed on the blankets.

His arm ached, but he did not think the wolf's teeth had punctured his heavy nylon parka. It had been too weak to attack, or maybe it was just a warning . . .

Jake was swept with a sickening sense of failure. 'I didn't stop Digger,' he groaned out loud. 'He would have shot me if it hadn't been for the white wolf! I've lost my snowshoes and left a trail that leads straight here!'

All Digger had to do was wait till dawn, and he could follow Jake straight to the shack. But Jake had to rest, just for a while . . . Before he knew it, Jake had fallen into a restless sleep.

'Imagine the wolves protecting Jake from Digger,' Jo sighed. 'Do you think that could be true?'

'Mr Bell heard the whole story from Jake,' Alex assured her. 'They were really protecting the white wolf that Digger shot. And of course, they knew Digger was their enemy.'

'Do you think the huge white wolf was the werewolf Digger was so frightened of . . . the one he thought he saw before?' Louise said.

'Read the journal,' Charlie suggested. 'See if Jake says anything.'

Alex picked up the journal and turned another stiff page. Her eyes scanned down the squiggly handwriting. 'Here it is . . .'

Monday morning, Feb. 6
I'm writing this in Lucy's shack. We survived the night. I say *we* because I woke up this morning to find Lucy sleeping beside me. She must have come in some time in the night. I wonder if she knows what happened to the white wolf . . .

'There's something strange going on,' Charlie said, staring at Alex.

'Wait. You don't know how strange,' Alex promised.

Eleven

'What did happen to the white wolf?' Louise asked. 'Did it die?'

'Maybe it was a ghost wolf, all along,' Charlie said. 'I mean, it *was* white, and it appeared out of nowhere to attack Digger and save Jake.'

'Don't talk about ghost *wolves*,' Louise shuddered. 'Ghosts were bad enough when they used to be human!'

Jo was peering down over the end of the couch.

'Pass me the candle,' she hissed to Alex. 'There's something down here.'

Alex passed the light, and Jo shone it on the floor, then jumped back. The sudden movement blew out the flame.

'Light it again!' she whispered. 'I saw something in my cereal bowl!'

They all hugged their feet underneath them, and waited while Alex opened the stove, stuck in a piece of cardboard from a cookie box, and used it as a torch to light the candle.

Then they bent over to look.

Sure enough, a small brown mouse with large ears was sipping delicately at the remains of the milk in Jo's dish.

'Oh, it's so cute,' Charlie cried. 'Look at its big brown eyes.'

'Shoo! Get out of there!' Jo waved her arms.

The mouse leapt lightly out of the bowl, leaving a tiny trail of wet footprints as it scampered away.

'I guess it wasn't such a good idea to leave our dishes on the floor,' Alex shook her head.

Just then, there was a crackle and a scramble, and a bag of pretzels began to skitter across the cabin floor.

'There are mice in the pretzels!' Charlie screamed, picking up the bag and dumping the pretzels and two more mice on to the floor. They scurried under the couch, their long tails waving.

'Now they've gone too far,' Charlie stood up, her hands on her hips, surveying the mess. 'Pretzels are my favourite.'

'Then you won't be too upset that they're also eating the caramel corn,' Jo pointed to a mouse perched on the edge of a box of sweet popcorn, nibbling at a plump kernel.

'I think I'd better get a broom,' Alex sighed, standing up. 'We'll never have any peace until we've cleaned up.'

'We should wash these dishes,' Louise said, gathering up the dirty bowls from the floor. 'Ugh! They've all had mice in them.'

'What are we going to wash them with?' Charlie asked. She looked around the dim, quiet cabin, 'Bottled water?'

It sank in suddenly that there was no hot water in the cabin, no running water at all, not even a kitchen sink. At that moment the cabin felt strange and unwelcoming, a hostile place. A wolf howl, far away and lonely, made them all fall silent, listening.

'I never thought I'd be sorry not to wash dishes . . .' Charlie began.

'We could get a pot of snow and melt it on the stove, like Jake and Lucy did,' Jo said at last.

'Sure. And go out in the blizzard, with the wolves, to get it?' Charlie said.

'Bad idea, I guess,' Jo shrugged. She brushed back a strand of her dark hair. 'Let's just put the dishes in a covered pot, and when Alex's parents get back, we'll wash them.'

They were quiet as they swept up the cabin. It was fine for Jo to talk about when Alex's parents got back, but they all knew it might be a long time until anyone got through the storm that was still raging outside.

'Waste of good pretzels . . .' Charlie muttered as she shook out the crumbs from their sleeping bags.

'Let's sit with our feet curled up underneath us,' Alex suggested. 'In case the mice run around our feet.'

'Let's hear some more about Jake,' Louise stammered. 'S-somehow, when I hear about how cold and desperate he is, I don't feel so bad about us.'

'Up in that dark little hut, with no windows, or furniture,' Jo agreed.

'And no food!' Charlie said. 'It was much worse than this.'

Alex nodded. 'Things were pretty awful for Jake.' She patted the notebook on her lap. 'The Bells were worried about him . . .'

Alex stared into space as she remembered the storekeeper's words. The others leaned forward to listen to her clear voice.

The Bells opened the store at nine on

Monday morning, and watched eagerly for Jake's parents' truck on the road.

But as the hours crawled by, there was no sign of the Kingstons.

'You should have insisted on seeing Jake last night,' Mrs Bell nagged. She screwed a lid down tightly on a candy jar. 'I wouldn't have left until I made sure he was all right.'

'Well, you should have gone up there yourself, then,' Mr Bell said. He was secretly ashamed of having been afraid of Digger. 'I should stick to my store,' he muttered to himself. 'It's always a mistake to get involved in other people's business.'

'Maybe we could both drive up a little later,' Mrs Bell said.

Up in Lucy's shack the same Monday morning, Jake moved slowly, trying to open the barrel stove without squeaking the door. Lucy was still asleep, and he didn't want to wake her.

But when Jake turned around, Lucy was watching him. Jake felt his heart lurch. Her face was so pale it was almost as white as the snow.

He waited for Lucy to speak but she just gazed at him with her strange, beautiful eyes.

'Would . . . would you like some tea?' he stammered, at last.

Lucy just nodded her head, and closed her eyes again.

Jake fed the fire until the barrel stove was glowing red hot, then set a pot of snow on top. It melted in a moment and was soon bubbling around the edges.

He threw in some tea, boiled it for a few seconds, and then poured the steaming tea in to an empty jam jar he'd been using for a mug.

'Here,' he said. 'Watch, it's hot.'

Lucy reached one arm out from under the blankets and took the jar. She sipped gratefully, without sitting up.

'Do you know what happened last night?' Jake asked. He had some explaining to do.

Lucy nodded. 'I saw the whole thing.' She swallowed a little more tea. It seemed to be hard for her to speak.

'Is the white wolf . . . all right?' Jake asked gently. Somehow, he was sure Lucy would know.

'She . . . will be OK,' she murmured. 'The others will look after her.'

'The other wolves?' Jake said.

Lucy nodded again, and closed her eyes.

'Do you think the others . . . killed Digger?'

Lucy rolled her head back and forth on the pillow.

'I hope not. If they kill a human, even a piece of scum like Digger, people will hunt them down until not one of them is left alive. That's what has happened everywhere else . . .'

Lucy gazed at him. Her eyes were filled with anger. 'You should have stayed here, and left Digger to me,' she exclaimed. 'Digger will come after you now. He knows you're alive. He will follow your trail. He'll see the smoke, and the blood on the snow . . .' She tried to rise. 'We should get out of here!'

'It's snowing right now,' Jake soothed. 'The snow should hide our tracks and the smoke.'

'He will be hunting us . . .' Lucy insisted. She tried to sit up again, but the colour faded from her face until it was ghastly white again, and she fell back on the blankets.

'What's the matter?' Jake went quickly and knelt beside her.

Lucy's teeth were tightly clenched and beads of cold sweat stood out on her forehead.

'My arm,' she muttered.

It was then Jake noticed bloodstains on Lucy's fur-trimmed parka, which had been thrown to one side.

He peeled back the grey wool blankets. Blood had soaked through the sleeve of Lucy's blue shirt.

Jake took out his pocketknife, and carefully cut the sleeve away from the wound. There was a nasty gash in her right arm, between the wrist and the elbow.

'How did you do this?' Jake demanded.

'I tore it on a tree branch,' Lucy muttered through her clenched teeth.

'It needs cleaning,' Jake said desperately. He had no bandages, no first aid equipment – nothing!

'We have to get you home,' Jake bent low near Lucy's ear. 'I mean – your foster home. There must be someone there who can look after you.'

Lucy's pale eyes were pools of loneliness. 'No,' she said. 'There isn't.'

Jake swallowed, and glanced away. He knew that look, that feeling. He had often felt lonely, without brothers or sisters and living in mining camps far from other kids his own age.

'What happened to your parents?' He blurted.

Lucy suddenly looked fierce. 'I have no parents. My mother died when I was eight. My dad had lots of girlfriends and two wives, but none of them wanted me around. I've lived in six foster homes. The one I'm in now is really bad. I stay here most of the time.'

'But this place . . .' Jake looked around.

'What's wrong with it?' Lucy frowned.

'Well, what do you eat? Where do you wash your clothes?'

'I have some money, and I . . . I hunt. I heat water to wash clothes. I'm old enough to get a job planting trees this year. Tree planters don't have to dress up, just work hard. I'm going to save money and build myself a bigger place.'

Lucy gazed around the tiny shack. 'But I won't tear this shack down. I like it because it reminds me of Ruby,' She glanced at Jake. 'Ruby taught me to hunt and snare rabbits. She taught me how to be free, not to ask anything of anybody.'

'But don't you want a home, or a family – when you get older?' Jake asked.

Lucy sighed. 'A home is just a jail. A family means you're too busy looking after kids to go outside. I can't live inside.'

'But what happens if you meet somebody

some day who wants to look after you?' Jake insisted.

'I've been waiting for years to be old enough to get away from all those people who say they want to look after me.' Lucy looked fierce again. 'I'm almost there—' She winced with pain and closed her eyes. 'I think I'll sleep now.'

Her eyes closed again and she drifted off to sleep.

Jake put some more wood in the stove and sat watching her. Despite Lucy saying she didn't want anyone to care about her, he did care. He was worried about her breathing. It didn't sound right.

Jake let her sleep for several hours, until she began to moan and thrash. Then he softly nudged her shoulder.

Lucy woke with a gasp. Her eyes looked wildly around. 'I dreamed Digger was here!' she cried. 'He found us—' She clutched his hand with her cold one.

'It's still snowing,' Jake said gently. 'But you need a doctor,' he urged.

Lucy sighed again and rolled away from him, hugging her arm. 'It's too far,' she whispered.

'Then what can I do?' Jake pleaded. 'There must be something I can do.'

'You could make me some soup,' Lucy said. 'There's frozen meat in the food locker, under the floor.' She pointed to a square saw cut in the floor boards.

Jake pried up the section of floor, and hauled out the food box. It was ice cold. The bones inside were frozen into a solid mass. They didn't seem to have much meat on them.

'Boil the whole thing with some snow,' Lucy murmured. 'It will be fine.'

Jake grabbed the pot and went outside to pack it full of snow. When he returned, he gasped at what he saw. Lucy had her back to him. She was holding her wounded arm up to her face. She was licking her wound!

Jake turned away quickly, pretending he hadn't seen. 'How long do I boil these – bones,' his voice came out a whisper.

Lucy rolled over and looked at him. He could see her hunger in her eyes.

'Just thaw them,' she said.

'Oh, yuck!' Charlie gagged. 'She wants to chew on raw bones!'

'That's the grossest thing I ever heard,' Louise shuddered. 'I don't even like to eat meat cooked.'

'But it's true,' Alex nodded. 'Mr Bell heard the whole story from Jake.'

'And imagine, licking your own cut,' Charlie went on. 'I think this girl has been hanging out with the wolves for too long!'

Twelve

'Why would Lucy keep bones in a box under the floor?' Jo's dark blue eyes were full of questions.

'That's pretty weird, too,' Charlie agreed.

'Well,' Alex explained, 'It's not really that weird – not up here. Lots of people have a cold storage hole dug into the ground under their floors. It keeps stuff cool in the summer and acts like a freezer in the winter. Don't forget – there's no electricity to run a refrigerator.'

'But a box? Full of bones?' Louise was still shuddering.

'The box would be metal to keep out the animals and bugs,' Alex shook her head. 'You guys sure are city wimps.'

'I don't care,' Louise shook her head. 'There is something very strange about Lucy.'

'Keep going,' Jo said. 'Tell us what happened next.'

* * *

So Alex hunkered forward, with her long, fine fingers clasped around her knees. As she began to speak, her words took them back to the dim interior of Lucy's shack.

Jake had put the chunk of frozen bones and meat in the pot on the stove with some fresh snow.

In a few minutes, the snow had melted on the hot fire.

Jake was poking at the frozen lump of meat, trying to separate the bones with a stick when he heard a strange sound behind him.

It was somewhere between a gasp and a growl.

When he turned around, Lucy was on her knees, her head thrust forward.

'Don't wait,' she said in a strange, low voice. 'Don't wait for them to cook.'

'But they're still raw and cold,' Jake said. 'I've barely got the ice out of them.'

'It doesn't matter. I need them now,' Lucy made that strange noise again. Her long, tangled hair had fallen forward over her face, and all Jake could see were her eyes, glowing with fever.

'You're sick,' he cried, trying to press her down on the pile of blankets. 'You have a fever, Lucy. You're hallucinating.'

Lucy shook her head. Her body was amazingly strong as Jake tried to get her to lie down under the covers again.

'No,' she cried hoarsely, 'I need to eat. I'm so weak. I'm so weak . . .'

'Just lie still,' Jake said. 'The meat will cook in just a little while.'

But he was scared. Lucy's eyes were wild and she fought him, crawling on all fours, reaching for a raw bone from the pot – hissing when the hot stove almost burned her hand – falling back on the bed with a red, dripping bone in her hand, barely thawed – sinking her teeth into it.

She's gone completely out of her mind, Jake thought in horror. His mind wouldn't let him imagine what other reason there could be for this terrifying change.

'Lucy, I'm going down the mountain,' he cried, reaching for her pack, for his hat and gloves. 'You need help. I think my parents will be back from the city by now. I'll get some first-aid supplies, and more food. Stay here, and try to stay warm.'

'Don't bring anyone back.' Lucy clutched at his hand. 'Promise you won't tell anyone where I am, or bring anyone here. Promise me.'

Jake was frightened by the look in her eyes.

'All right,' he said. 'I promise.'

He found Lucy's snowshoes outside and strapped them on his own boots. The snow was still falling heavily. If only it would keep up until his parents got back, until they got help!

He started off, snowshoeing through the pines as if his life depended on it, not liking to think about Lucy, alone in the shack.

He had reached the edge of the woods when he heard the sharp CRACK! of a broken branch. He flattened himself against the snow behind a low-growing pine.

It was Digger, impatiently breaking off the branches in his way. He was snowshoeing along the ridge, his rifle slung over his shoulder.

Jake lay, barely breathing, watching the man. Digger was nervous. He kept glancing over his shoulder, giving a start when he thought he heard something, swinging his rifle forward. He was as dangerous as a stick of dynamite on a short fuse, Jake thought.

Digger prowled back and forth along the top of the ridge. He seemed to be watching the road on the other side, the road down the mountain to Bell's Store.

He's smart, Jake thought. He doesn't know where I am, but he knows where I want to go. Digger must be desperate. It would be no use rigging an 'accident' for his parents while he was still alive.

Jake knew he was being hunted as surely as any wild game.

Digger turned and scanned the woods again, as if he sensed he was being watched. Jake flattened his face against the snow. He felt fear crawl down his back and tighten his breathing. Digger was just a few paces away. If he came through those trees . . .

It was not safe to move a muscle.

Jake lay rigid, until the cold seeped through his clothing and into his bones, until his eyes felt heavy and his body numb.

He pinched himself awake. Lying still in the cold was dangerous. How long, he wondered, before he froze?

An hour later, he could hardly feel his thumb and finger when he tried to pinch his own face. Soon he would have to move. It was better to try to run than to freeze to death.

All at once he heard Digger's familiar cursing.

'That bloody fool Bell! What does he want this time!'

Jake raised his head. Digger was staring down at the road. The he turned and marched away towards the mine, his face a twisted mask of fury.

'Saved by the Bells,' Jake breathed. He felt relief rise like a giddy bubble in his chest. He waited until Digger was out of sight, then rose painfully to his feet and started back towards Lucy's shack. He was tired, starving and chilled to the bone. Now that he knew Digger was hunting him, he knew he would have to be more careful. With this in mind, Jake broke off a thick evergreen branch and dragged it behind him, trying to brush out his trail through the snow.

There was no trickle of smoke from the shack's stove pipe. The fire must be out.

'Lucy!' Jake called, as he flung the curtain aside and fell to his knees to look in.

It was cold as death inside the shack.

Jake fumbled with his snowshoes, untying the harness, kicking his feet free. 'Lucy!' he called urgently. 'I'm back.'

She was still breathing, deep asleep in the mound of blankets. Her face felt cold to his touch.

He must get her warm! Jake stuffed branches into the cold ashes of the stove, stuck a curl of birch bark under the wood and lit a match. The bark crackled and caught fire instantly, and blazed up through the balsam branches.

The pot of bones and meat was empty. Lucy must have eaten every scrap. Shuddering, Jake scooped some clean snow to boil water, and set it on the hottest part of the stove. He sat beside Lucy and rubbed her cold hands with his own.

'Lucy,' he whispered in her cold ear, 'wake up!'

He gave her shoulder a little shake.

To his great relief, Lucy's eyelids fluttered and she twitched and groaned in her sleep. She was conscious!

Jake put more wood in the stove, building the fire as hot as he dared. He knew it was important to get some warm liquid into both of them, to warm them from the inside, too.

'I'm going to look at your arm.' He pulled back the blankets. Surprisingly, the wound seemed better. The licking must have helped . . .

Jake shuddered again, not just with cold. Imagine licking your own wound, like an animal! Lucy opened her blue eyes and blinked at him. She held up her injured arm as if it was some strange object she'd never seen before.

'I've got the fire going again,' Jake stammered. 'I'll make you some tea.'

'Jake,' Lucy stopped him. She looked wildly around. 'What time is it?'

'It's almost five,' Jake said. 'It's all right. It will soon be dark and Digger won't be able to see our smoke.'

Lucy stared at him with startled eyes. 'Dark, so soon?' she said in a hoarse voice. 'I have to go . . .' She tried to sit up, but Jake held her back.

'Wait,' he urged. 'You've been sleeping all day. You're chilled to the bone. You're safe here, and you need to warm up, and . . .'

'No!' Lucy shook her head, and her long hair whipped in her face. 'I have to go. I can't stay.' She was shivering violently.

'You're so cold,' Jake said helplessly.

'I'll just have some tea, then I'll go.' Lucy sank back on the blankets.

Jake made the tea, and handed it to her.

She looked calmer, and the colour was coming back to her cheeks as the shelter grew warmer. Her eyes pierced Jake, as she gazed at him over the lip of the steaming jar.

'Jake,' she said. 'How is your arm? Did the bite, did the teeth . . . puncture the skin?'

Jake suddenly remembered the wolf's

teeth, clamped on his arm. It hadn't been hurting, but when he looked at his left parka sleeve there were puncture holes. He unzipped his parka and shook it off his left arm. Under the sleeve of his shirt were small purple bruises in two neat rows, from his wrist almost to his elbow.

Lucy grabbed his arm and looked closely at the marks, then let it drop with a sigh. 'No,' she said. 'There's no dried blood – your skin wasn't broken. She didn't mean to bite you. It was just the pain.' She sighed again, and lay back on the blankets.

Jake stared at Lucy. She sounded almost sad that he hadn't been more seriously hurt. And how did she know about the wolf fastening her teeth on his arm last night?

He was suddenly overwhelmed with everything that was happening. It was all so strange and horrible. Digger had tried to kill him – was still trying to kill him. His parents were in danger and he and Lucy were trapped in this tiny shack in the wilderness. Somehow he must try to keep them all safe, especially Lucy. He realised that she mattered more to him than all the rest.

'Please stay,' he whispered.

'I'd like to . . .' She held up her slender hand, and Jake clasped it.

'Lucy, what's happening to you? I should go for help . . .'

'It's too late. I can't go back. Please, Jake, don't go for help. They'll lock me up in a place for crazy people. I'll die. I have to be free.'

Jake saw the wild pleading in Lucy's eyes. He suddenly knew she was right. It was too late for human help.

'I promise you, I'll be safe. I have things . . . I have to do, Lucy said softly. 'And you must promise me that whatever you do, you won't follow me, or try to find me.'

Jake stared back at Lucy. He couldn't let her go out in the darkness and cold. 'You're too weak,' he stumbled over his words. 'You've been hurt . . .'

Lucy's eyes flashed. 'I'm much stronger than I look,' she told him. 'I will be fine. But you have to promise not to follow me,' she begged again. 'Otherwise, it will be the last time you ever see me.'

Jake was silent for a moment. He couldn't force her to stay against her will. 'I guess I have no choice,' he muttered. 'But stay away from Digger. This is not your battle.'

'Digger is my enemy, too,' Lucy's eyes blazed again. 'He has known that for a long

100

time.' She reached for her parka, and got unsteadily to her feet.

'I will try to see you tomorrow.' Lucy winced as she pulled on her coat. Jake looked away. This was too painful to watch. Lucy was staggering, she was so weak. The colour had flooded out of her cheeks when she stood, leaving her pale as a ghost.

'Don't follow me,' she said hoarsely, and then she was gone.

Somewhere, off to the north, a wolf began to howl.

She would freeze to death out there, Jake thought. She was almost too weak to stand, let alone wade through deep snow. Had she even taken her snowshoes?

He pulled back the curtain to look.

The moon had already risen over the pointed tops of the evergreen trees. It rode, pale and perfectly round, in a cloudless sky.

Lucy's snowshoes were still leaning against the shelter.

Her trail snaked away from the shack, a weaving, stumbling channel through the snow.

How far could she get in that deep powder?

'I was crazy to let her go!' Jake told himself. 'I have to go after her!'

A lone wolf howl sounded from the right, and then the left. As long as they lasted, Jake could not move. It was a sound that reached down inside and made you tremble like the smallest mouse, cowering in its tunnel under the snow.

'I hate to say it,' Alex stood up. 'But we're going to need more firewood.'

Louise looked horrified. 'But that means going outside.'

Alex rattled the empty wood box. 'We don't want the stove to go out,' she told them. 'I don't know how to start it again.'

'We could burn the furniture,' Charlie said cheerfully. 'I saw that in a movie once.'

Jo wriggled out from under her bag and hurried, shivering, to join Alex. 'The thermometer says thirty-five below zero out there,' she shuddered. 'I think we should try to keep the stove going.'

'Come on,' Alex said. 'Charlie and I will go. Four or five logs each – that should get us through the night.'

'But the wolves . . .' Louise protested, her face pale. As if on cue, the howl of a wolf sent them all into shivers of silence. It was a long, mournful howl that made the hair stand up on the backs of their necks.

'It's too dangerous,' Jo shook her head.

'I'll open the door,' Alex said calmly. 'If I see anything, I'll slam it shut. If it looks clear, Charlie and I will make a run for the woodpile.'

Thirteen

Alex and Charlie were dressed and ready in their parkas, mitts, boots and hats.

'I don't think the wolves will eat me,' Charlie said bravely. 'I'm just one big blob of synthetic fibres!'

Alex cautiously tugged at the door.

This time it didn't fly open in her face. The storm had settled into a thick curtain of falling snow, but there was a drift in the doorway as deep as their knees.

They plunged into the darkness and snow, Alex leading the way.

'Don't go so fast,' Charlie called. 'The drifts are so deep, I can't walk straight.'

'Well, stay on your feet,' Alex bellowed. 'Don't flounder around like some wounded deer when there are wolves out here.'

Through the sheet of falling snow, Charlie thought she glimpsed a dark shape. 'Alex! Alex, I see something!' she screamed. 'It's coming closer! ALEX!!'

'It's me, you idiot,' Alex plunged up to Charlie. 'Here. Take these inside. I'm going back for more.' She dumped her load of split logs in Charlie's arms. 'Just keep the door open for me.'

Charlie dived back to the door and launched herself, wood and all, into a skid that took her halfway across the floor. A few seconds later, Alex came crashing through the door behind her, and there was firewood and snow and a tangle of bodies on the cabin floor.

'Shut the door!' They all screamed at once. Somehow, the door was banged shut and they lay in a heap, breathing hard.

'We did it,' Charlie said at last. 'We got the wood.'

'You were a big help,' Alex groaned.

'Did I hear some cries of terror from the great tease herself out there?' Jo asked Charlie.

'Maybe I was a bit afraid,' Charlie admitted. She stood up and brushed the snow out of her hair. 'But I saw something – a grey shape, sort of wavering . . .'

Alex nodded. 'I think there are wolves,' she agreed. 'We should stay in from now on – we've got enough wood.'

Ten minutes later, a hot fire was roaring

in the stove, and all four of them were round it in a half-circle, wrapped in their sleeping bags.

Louise was glad the cabin was getting warmer. She hadn't wanted to complain before, but she had been freezing! 'Tell us what happened, Alex,' she shivered. 'Did Jake find Lucy?'

'Yes, but not in the way he expected,' Alex said. For once, her sensible voice seemed to chill them to the bone.

Alex took up the story with a slight shiver of her own. 'He found Lucy, all right.' Her eyebrows were two upside-down Vs as she stared into the fire and her voice sank.

Jake put on Lucy's snowshoes and hurried to do up the harness. He didn't like the sound of those wolves so close.

Lucy called herself a friend of the wolves, but she was wounded and weak. She had said herself that it was a wolf's instinct to hunt the weak animals – to cut them out of the herd. Now, her own trail was the trail of a helpless doe, staggering, with here and there a deep impression where she had fallen over.

There! He could see her now, ahead of him, her white parka clear in the light of the full moon.

Jake put on a burst of speed. The wolves were closing in. Out of the corner of his eyes he could see their slim grey shapes, slipping in and out of the moonlit shadows.

Lucy was heading straight for a dense thicket of balsam trees, like the one in which she had built the shelter. Before Jake could reach her she had disappeared under the branches.

Jake stopped. Between him and the thicket, grey shapes were gathering. Jake's heart thudded in his chest. They looked like the same seven wolves that had surrounded Digger. He didn't dare to go closer.

Eerily, without making a sound, the wolves formed a circle in the snow, as though they were waiting for something. Then out of the thicket, and into the centre of the circle bounded a pure white wolf. Her fur glimmered in the moonlight. She threw back her head, opened her throat and howled. The others joined in the fearsome chorus to the moon.

It was a beautiful, but terrible sight. Jake felt a thick fear gather in the back of his throat. Where was Lucy?

The wolves began to stream away, running in a pack. The white wolf ran with them. She was limping in her right foreleg, injured in exactly the same place as Lucy was wounded in her arm.

All at once a chill swept over Jake, so deep he almost sank to his knees. Lucy was the white wolf. Jake had known it all day, but couldn't make himself admit it. Even now, his common sense fought against the idea. He had to be sure.

Jake raced forward on Lucy's snowshoes. He dived into the dense thicket of balsam, where Lucy had vanished.

'Lucy, are you here?' he called. He thrashed his way through the branches. They whipped his face and stopped his progress, but he fought through, to the very heart of the thicket. There he found an ancient cedar tree, with a hollow in the middle.

A sliver of moonlight shone into the cavity in the tree. There was something white inside.

Jake shoved his hand in the hole.

It was cloth – Lucy's coat. He recognised the fur trimming around the hood. As he pulled it out, the rest of her clothes, bundled inside, fell into the snow.

Jake felt a dark hand over his heart. Lucy must come here to be transformed into a wolf. She left her clothes in the hollow tree, until morning.

Jake stuffed the clothes back into the hollow tree. He wormed his way out of the thicket. Far off, he could hear the wolves calling to each other. He set off, following the trail of the pack. They were running, close together.

Now the howl changed. They had caught the scent of a deer, and were running her to exhaustion in the deep snow. The deer was helpless on her long thin legs. A wolf's paws were designed to run over the top of the snow.

Jake had not gone very far down the ridge when he heard a final howl of triumph, clear and strong on the night air. The wolves sang that the deer lay dead on the snow, that now the wolves could eat.

Jake stopped, sucking in huge lungfuls of the cold night air. Was Lucy part of this, too? He went on down the ridge until he overlooked the kill. The body of the deer lay in a clearing. Her blood looked black on the trampled snow; the wolves were grey shadows, except for one white wolf whose coat shone silver in the moonlight.

The wolves were feasting, tearing at the flesh of the deer. The white wolf joined in the feast.

Jake did not go closer. He did not want to see any more. Sick at heart, he turned in a wide circle, and headed back on his own trail to the shack. He would keep the fire burning, and wait all night if he had to, for Lucy to return.

At last, when it was almost morning, he curled up under the blankets and fell asleep.

But when Jake opened his eyes and crawled out of the shack, he was alone.

Outside, the sky was blanketed with winter cloud. Jake saw a white world, with even the dark evergreens drooping under thick cloaks of soft snow.

Out of this white, silent world stepped the white wolf. Jake didn't see her at first, she blended so well with the background.

When he did see her, he was not afraid.

The white wolf just stood looking at him, calm and dignified. Her slanted blue eyes had a fierce, intelligent expression, as if she would like to speak.

'Lucy?' Jake whispered.

The wolf whined, and turned away. Suddenly she stopped and gave him a look over her shoulder that went straight to his heart. It was a look that was both sad and accusing at the same time. Then, she padded away towards the forest.

Jake felt his head whirl. Lucy had said 'If you follow me, you'll never see me again.'

And he had promised *not* to follow.

And he had broken that promise.

Jake sank down in the snow. Lucy had left every night, to run with the wolf pack. She had come back every day at dawn as a girl. But it was morning, and she was still in the wolf's body. What had he done?

A terrible feeling of loneliness swept over Jake. Lucy had been his friend. He had been able to talk to her like no one he had ever known. And he had betrayed her, and lost her.

Rising quickly to his feet, Jake stumbled back to the shack. He snatched up the snowshoes and headed down the mountain towards the Crossroads Store. Maybe he had been imagining things. Maybe he would find Lucy there, buying supplies. Maybe the Bells had seen her. He had to find out.

'Oh, wow,' Jo said. 'Do you think Jake saw what he thought he saw?'

'What other explanation could there be?'

Louise shuddered. 'Lucy is the white wolf, the werewolf.'

'Jake might be hallucinating,' Charlie said. 'He might have been so hungry and strung out he was imagining things. I get like that when I'm hungry.'

'How do you ever get hungry?' Louise raised her eyebrows. 'You're always eating.'

'Why do you think she wanted to know if the wolf's teeth had broken Jake's skin?' Jo wondered. 'That part made me feel creepy.'

'It's an old werewolf legend,' Alex told her. 'If a werewolf bites you, you become a werewolf too.'

'So then she and Jake could have been wolves together,' Jo said dreamily, 'but she wouldn't have bitten him on purpose. She liked him too much. Look in the journal,' Jo waved her hand at the book on the arm of Alex's chair. 'Did Jake write anything about what happened that night?'

Alex held the book close to the candle to look, but the candle flame was drowning in its own pool of melted wax.

'This is our last candle,' Alex pulled the stub of a red candle out of her pocket. She lit it from the dying flame of the quickly-melting candle. 'After this, we'll be telling stories in the dark.'

'Don't say that,' Louise whispered. 'There isn't even a street light outside. It will be pitch-black in here.'

'We'll still have the fire,' Jo reminded her. 'Go ahead, Alex, see what Jake says in the journal.'

Alex held the crackling paper up to the candle flame. 'OK, listen.'

Tuesday morning, Feb. 7
I'm afraid I'll never see her again, like she said. I broke my promise . . . But I'm not going to stop looking for her. I'm sure she wouldn't hurt me. It's just Digger that she hates. He represents everything evil and destructive. I have to protect her from Digger.

'He doesn't care if she's a werewolf,' Jo cried. 'He still loves her!'

Fourteen

'Tell us what happened,' Charlie said, swinging her legs over the end of the couch. 'Did Lucy ever come back?' For once, she had forgotten to eat.

'I want to listen for another weather report, first,' Alex said. 'Not that I'm worried, or anything, but it *is* getting close to midnight . . .'

'Ah,' Charlie grinned. She reached for the CD player on the floor, and swung it over to Alex. 'Midnight, the hour of werewolves and vampires.'

'This could be one of those three-day blizzards,' Jo said. 'We could be up on the mountain all week, and miss school . . .'

'Stop that!' Louise cried.

'Quiet a second . . . I'm getting something.' Alex held up her hand.

But the radio crackled and hissed as static drowned the signal.

'How do you stand it?' Charlie asked

Alex. 'I mean, being so cut off up here?'

'Is our fearless one getting nervous?' Jo asked.

'Well, I'd just like to hear the end of this story. I mean it *did* happen right here, on this mountain, where we happen to be stranded, and that Digger person, slept in this cabin . . . ugh!' Charlie shivered at the thought.

'How about some music?' Alex suggested. 'We have our CDs.'

'Good idea.' Jo reached for the case of discs. 'How about *Wolf Songs*?' She glanced from one to the other. 'It seems kind of appropriate.'

The music filled the cabin.

'Turn it down a bit,' Charlie said, 'so we can hear Alex.'

The music died to a background murmur. Alex leaned forward again, watching the colours dance in the flames, blue, yellow and red, as she went on.

Jake set out to see if he could find any trace of Lucy. When he came to the edge of the forest, Jake shook off his feeling of being part of a strange, magical world. His senses switched to a state of high alert. This is where he'd heard the branch crack, and seen Digger,

115

the day before. Digger was probably still patrolling the ridge and the road below, more desperate to find him than ever!

Jake planned to take a roundabout route to the store, avoiding the road. He cut through the bush, snowshoeing hard, and came up to the Crossroads Store from the back.

Inside their store, the Bells were leaning on the counter.

'Well,' Mrs Bell smiled. 'It's a relief to see you, Jake Kingston. Mr Bell and I have been worried.'

'Have you seen . . . Lucy?' Jake panted.

Mrs Bell's face clouded over. 'No, I have not. And neither has anyone else, apparently, for quite some time. Would you like to tell us what's been going on up there with you two?'

Mr Bell broke in. 'I was just going to drive up to the mine with a message for you, Jake.'

'From my parents?'

'That's right,' Mrs Bell nodded. 'They said to tell you they have some more banking to do, but they ought to be back tomorrow. I guess a big gold deal like that takes a lot of arranging.'

'I guess . . .' Jake said. What did it matter? The important thing was that his parents weren't coming back. Somehow, he had to get through another day and a night without their help!

He headed for the door.

'Will you be going back up to the mine?' Mrs Bell asked.

'N-no,' Jake stammered. 'I haven't been staying at the mine, lately.'

Mr and Mrs Bell shot each other meaningful looks. 'Do you need help, son?' Mr Bell asked kindly.

'Maybe . . .' Jake said. 'Could I talk to you – privately?'

'Why don't we go out in the garage?' Mr Bell slowly came out from behind the counter and put a hand on Jake's shoulder.

'Lucy's disappeared,' Jake said, when they had got out of range of Mrs Bell's sharp ears. 'I'm worried about her.'

'I wouldn't be too concerned,' Mr Bell shook his head. 'She's done this before. If I were you, I'd go and ask Ruby LaFleur if she's seen Lucy.'

Mr Bell pointed to the ramshackle grey wood house a short distance down the road. 'She lives right over there,' he said. 'If anyone knows where Lucy is, it will be Ruby.'

'Thanks, Mr Bell,' Jake said. 'It . . . it isn't like Mrs Bell thinks,' Jake stammered.

Mr Bell shook his head. 'You'd be a darn

sight better off not to get mixed up with that girl,' he said. 'What do you want me to tell your parents, if I see them before you do?'

'Please ask them to wait for me here at the store,' Jake said quickly. 'Tell them I need to talk to them.'

Mr Bell nodded. 'I can do that.'

'And one more thing. Don't tell Digger you've seen me, if he comes into the store.'

Mr Bell looked worried. 'Are you sure you don't need help?'

If he got the Bells involved, that would mean the police, the authorities. He'd have no chance to be alone at the shack. No chance to see Lucy, in case she came back.

'No,' he said finally. 'Just give my mum and dad my message, thanks.'

Mr Bell shook his head. 'Good luck, young fellow,' he said. 'I'll do what I can.'

Jake tore across the road and down to the small grey house. When nobody answered his knock, he opened the door and bellowed, 'Ms LaFleur? I've come about Lucy!'

The house smelled of fried onions and old paper, and was piled high with newspapers and magazines.

'Come in,' he heard a gravelly voice. 'Let me see who just opens my door and lets in the cold.'

Jake shut the door quickly. He walked through a narrow corridor in the piles of papers to the kitchen, where Ruby sat in her wheelchair, eating her lunch.

It was steak and fried onions.

Suddenly, Jake was overwhelmed by hunger. It was hours since he'd eaten.

'Pull up a chair,' Ruby growled in her hoarse old voice. She had iron-grey hair and a lined face, but her eyes were bright and inquisitive. She pushed the plate of meat and onions over to his side of the table. 'It looks like you could use a bite or two. Tell me about my girl.'

It was only after gulping down a huge chunk of steak, and telling Ruby the entire story of the events of the past few days that Jake glanced down and saw Ruby's folded and pinned pant legs perched on the pads of the wheelchair.

'It's not so bad as you think,' Ruby smiled at him. 'I'm alive, thanks to that girl, and that's a darn sight better than being dead.'

'About Lucy . . .' Jake reminded her.

Ruby shook her head. There was sorrow in her deep-set eyes. 'I have heard many legends about the *loup-garou*, the werewolf. She's not always evil. Sometimes the soul of a person, the best part, can run with the wolves, they say. But always, she protects her secret. They say that once you go after her, and find where she hides her human clothes, she can't come back.'

'She told me not to follow, but I was so worried about her . . .' Jake hung his head, tears stinging his eyes.

'Maybe those old stories are wrong,' Ruby said. 'Anyway. You bring that white wolf to me, if you can. Maybe there's something we can do, eh?'

Jake scraped back his chair and stood up. 'Thank you,' he said. 'I'll try to bring her.'

Ruby held up her hand. 'If she won't come, there's one more thing you can try.' She pointed to her own forehead. 'You split the skin between her eyes. Right here.' She drew an imaginary line from her hairline to the bridge of her nose. 'Sometimes, they say, the human body can be released, if you do that.'

Jake just stared at her. How could he cut the wolf between the eyes?

'Of course,' Ruby went on, 'she would have to have a powerful reason to return. Something calling her. Poor Lucy. I'm afraid life has not been very good to her. There's very little to bring her back.'

'She might come back to me,' Jake said quietly.

'Ah, yes.' Ruby beamed. 'Love is a power-ful force.' Then her face clouded. 'But so is hate. From what you have been telling me, I can't say if Lucy would want to stop being a wolf until her work is done.'

'You mean Digger?' Jake asked.

Ruby nodded. 'That's what I mean. She has many reasons to hate him.'

'And he hates the white wolf. He'll kill her if he has a chance.' Jake stood up. 'I'll try to bring her here. Thanks for the food.' He left the little grey house on the run, careful to close the door behind him.

Mrs Bell was looking out the window. 'There goes Jake like a bat out of a chimney, straight up the mountain again,' she said. 'Mr B, do you know what's going on?'

'No more than you,' Mr Bell shook his head. 'But there's something fishy about that Digger Grimes, that's for sure. Keep your eyes and ears open, Mrs B, and your mouth closed.'

'As if I didn't,' Mrs Bell laughed. She gave her round husband an affectionate hug. They looked like two barrels, embracing. 'As if we didn't both keep a sharp look-out.'

Fifteen

'Here comes Digger, spinning his wheels, as usual,' Mrs Bell said, an hour or so later. 'Are you going to stand up to him this time, Mr B?'

'I always stand up to him,' Mr Bell said indignantly. But he looked anxious as the green pickup skidded to a stop on the packed snow and Digger marched into the Crossroads Store.

'Have you seen the Kingston kid?' he demanded, fixing the Bells with his bloodshot eyes.

'Good morning, Mr Grimes,' Mrs Bell said, not looking up from her accounts. 'Anything we can do for you today?'

'I *said*, have you seen Jake?' Digger bellowed. 'Are you deaf?'

'We are not a news service.' Mr Bell was straightening cans on the shelf behind the counter. 'And I don't see that Jake's business is your business.'

'You don't? His parents left me in charge of him, that's all,' Digger shot back.

'Well, I can't say you're doing a very good job of being in charge of the boy if you don't even know where he is,' Mrs Bell sniffed.

'This is useless!' Digger slammed his dirty fist on the counter. 'Oh well, it doesn't matter anyway. I found out where the little sneak has been hiding out.'

The Bells stared at him.

'Oh, that got your attention!' Digger sneered. 'Yeah, he's been sleeping in a shack up on the ridge. I saw smoke coming from up there this morning. It was just a makeshift place, about the size of a shipping crate.'

Digger smiled, a horrible, filthy-toothed grin. 'A couple of good kicks,' he said, 'and that shack was a few sticks of lumber and sheets of tin.'

The Bells were still staring.

'Don't worry,' Digger laughed. 'The kid wasn't in the shack when I kicked it to pieces. That's why I thought I'd come looking for him. So, did you see him?'

The Bells glanced quickly at each other. Then they both pressed their lips together and shook their heads.

On the other side of the counter, Digger

looked furious. But there was no way the Bells were going to unseal those closed mouths.

Digger grunted and spun away. At the door he stopped and glared at them. 'Don't trouble yourselves,' he growled. 'I'll find Jake myself. You give him that message, if you see him. *I will find him.*'

Jake stared at the ruins of Lucy's shack, his breath coming in ragged gasps. The place had been savagely torn apart, and the grey blankets thrown over the stove. They still smoked and smouldered, throwing off a horrible, burnt-wool stench.

'Digger!' Jake muttered under his breath. Digger had done this, he was certain.

But it was he, Jake, who had left the fire burning, making an easy path for Digger to follow.

Jake sank to his knees in the snow. It was all his fault. And now, Lucy had no safe shelter. He realised that he had somehow counted on her coming back to this place she had been so proud of. It was a link with her human self, and now it was destroyed. Fury rose up in him.

Digger had kicked and twisted the tin roof so it could never be straightened. He had bashed in the stovepipe with a two-by-four. There had been hate behind this attack – hate directed at him, at Jake Kingston.

The CRACK! of a distant rifle shot made Jake leap to his feet. Terrified, he listened to it echo from one mountain face to another, knowing that it could only come from one direction. Digger – and the mine!

Jake had never snowshoed so fast. He raced down the ridge, seeming to hear the gunshot still echoing in his brain. 'Not Lucy!' he prayed. 'Please don't let it be the white wolf!'

He heard the generators before he reached the mine. Their pulsing noise seemed to fill the white silence like an insult. Jake realised, as he looked down at the mine, how much he hated that noise.

Digger's truck was parked by the gate, but there was no sign of the man.

Jake plunged the rest of the way down the ridge, took off his snowshoes and threw open the cabin door. 'DIGGER!' he roared. 'Are you in here?'

There was only cold silence in the cabin.

Jake turned to the mine entrance. It, too, looked deserted. But as Jake stuck his head in the dim cavernous entrance, he could hear a sound under the pounding of the

125

pump motors. It was a whine of pain, of protest.

He went a little further down the tunnel towards the sound. The tunnel was dimly lit with bare light bulbs strung on wires from the ceiling.

There was something white in the dimness – the white wolf, tied to a concrete block in the tunnel.

'Lucy!' Jake fell to his knees, trying to undo the snare-wire biting cruelly into her sore leg.

The wolf's lips suddenly bared in a frightening snarl. Her white teeth glinted in the dim light, her eyes glowed with hate.

Jake shrunk back, terrified. But the wolf's eyes were fixed on something behind him.

A shape stepped out of the shadows. It was Digger, mean and filthy in his green canvas coat and tool belt. He looked like he hadn't shaved in a week, Jake thought. An ugly sneer twisted his lip.

His evil laugh echoed down the tunnel. 'Better not get too close, Jake. She doesn't like us, not at all. She bit my hand while I was doing up that snare wire around her leg.' He held up a hand wrapped in a dirty piece of cloth.

'I thought that rifle shot might get you

down here,' Digger laughed again. 'But I didn't count on catching her too. She stepped right into one of the snares I set.'

The white wolf's snarl was a rumbling growl of hate coming from deep in her chest.

'Let her go!' Jake said furiously.

'Oh, no!' Digger shook his head. 'I'm not letting either of you go. I found this dynamite stuffed in the corner of your little shack and it made me mad all over again to think how you messed up my homecoming surprise for your mum . . . and dad.'

Digger hiccuped drunkenly. He swayed on his feet. He was clutching the dynamite to his chest, and trailing a long fuse. Jake was filled with loathing and disgust, partly at himself. He had forgotten all about the dynamite.

'So,' Digger went on, 'I thought we'd just start all over again. Rig up a little welcome home party for mummy and daddy, and Jake and the great big bad wolf . . .'

The white wolf pulled back her lips and growled again.

Digger jerked the rock hammer out of his tool belt. 'Growl at me, will you?' he shouted, and hurled the pointed hammer at the wolf.

She tried to leap aside, but the hammer caught her a glancing blow between the eyes. She yelped with pain.

'That'll teach you to—' Digger yelled.

He never finished. Jake sprang at him with all the fury in his heart. Behind him he could hear the white wolf howl with pain as she tried to join the attack and was jerked back by the steel wire.

But her cry threw Digger off balance. He staggered backwards, at the same time as he launched a blow at Jake's chest that sent him sprawling.

Behind Digger was a wide open hole – a deep shaft to the lower level of the mine.

Digger teetered on the edge of the hole, a look of fear and surprise on his face, and then fell, backwards, into the darkness, still holding the dynamite.

Jake threw his body forward to peer down the hole. In a split second he saw that Digger had fallen through his own web of electrical wires. A broken wire was fizzing and sparking in the darkness. At any second the dynamite could blow!

Jake threw himself back down the tunnel away from the shaft. He curled his body into a tight ball.

The explosion, when it came, rocked the

whole tunnel. Small chunks of loose rock thudded into his body. The air was filled with choking dust.

Then, from the dark hole below, came the shuddering howl of a wolf in torment. It was more terrible than any sound Jake had ever heard. The howl echoed horribly up and down the tunnels below.

Jake blocked his ears, thinking at first it was one of the wolves from the den, caught in the explosion. But the wolf tunnels had been sealed off by Digger's first explosion.

This was something else – something not human, and not animal. Jake crept to the edge of the shaft. He peered into the smoke-filled darkness. Digger's body was somewhere down there in the rubble. Or was it? The howls of rage and pain went on and on . . .

Jake heard a whimper and spun around. He had forgotten the white wolf, still cruelly tied to the concrete block.

Jake gasped. The skin on her forehead had been split open by the blow from Digger's hammer – between her eyes white bone gleamed through the blood-soaked fur.

Desperately, Jake bent over to undo the snare-wire that fastened her leg to the block. This time, the white wolf whined in her throat but did not snarl. Limping and bleeding, she followed Jake to the mine entrance.

'Run!' he shouted with all his strength. 'Go to Ruby – run!'

The wolf began to run towards the woods at the edge of the mine clearing. She was running oddly, Jake saw, and it was not just the wound. Her shape was changing, her body seemed taller as she disappeared into the trees. Or was it only his imagination?

'Holy whiskers!' Jo gasped. They were all silent, picturing the scene. The smoking mine shaft, the rubble in the tunnel, Jake watching Lucy vanish into the woods.

'Is there anything more in Jake's journal?' Louise gasped.

Alex flipped through the pages. 'No,' she said. 'But there's more to the story.'

Sixteen

'Wait,' Charlie cried. 'I need a chocolate bar
for this.' She jumped off the couch and dug
to the bottom of the food bag. 'Here,' she
called, tossing a bar to each of the others.

'How could Jake just let the white wolf
run away, hurt like that?' Louise said
indignantly.

'I think he was a little scared,' Jo said. 'I
know I would be.'

'How about you, Louise? Could it be
that you're not so scared of wolves as you
were before?' Charlie looked laughingly at
her friend.

'Well, not this wolf,' Louise protested.
'This is Lucy. He had to try to get her back.
He couldn't just go away, could he?'

They were all quiet for a moment, looking
around the cabin that had been Jake's home.

Alex opened the door and poked the
glowing fire. A shower of sparks, like
fireflies released from a jar, flew from a

burning log. Alex quickly shut the glass door again and sank back in her chair as she resumed the story.

The others leaned forward, eager to hear the end.

'This is what happened, at least the way the Bells told it to me,' Alex said. She began to speak, her voice eager.

Jake's strength was almost gone. But once more, he strapped on the snowshoes and climbed the ridge. He was headed for the thicket, where Lucy had hidden her clothes.

They were still there, stuffed in the hollow tree. Jake tied them into a bundle with the cord from his parka hood and set out for Ruby's.

He chose a route that didn't take him past the window of Bell's Store. The last thing he needed was Mrs Bell wondering what he was doing with Lucy's clothing.

Half an hour later he was tapping at Ruby's back door.

'Come round the front,' she called from inside. 'I don't use the back door in winter.'

Jake staggered round to the front of the house, glancing quickly up and down the road. He slipped through the front door.

'Is that you, Jake?' Ruby called from beyond the kitchen. 'You'd better come in here.'

With fear in his heart at what he would find, Jake walked through the dark rooms to a lighted bedroom.

He stopped in the doorway.

Lucy lay in the bed, with her long hair, now silvery grey, spread out on the pillow. An ugly gash scarred her white forehead. Her eyes were closed and a white sheet was pulled up over the bottom half of her face.

'Hush,' Ruby said. 'Don't wake her.'

Ruby was sitting quietly in her wheelchair on the other side of the bed, a basin of water on her lap.

'It's almost over,' Ruby whispered.

Jake saw one of Lucy's hands twitch violently under the sheet. He looked away. The movement had looked too much like an animal, scratching.

'Is she . . .? Will she be all right?' Jake stammered.

Ruby shook her head, slowly. 'I think so,' she murmured, 'but it's been a hard struggle for her. She must have wanted to come back.' Ruby smiled. 'I think love won.'

Jake sank down beside the bed. He thought of all that had happened in the last few days. Had they really won?

'Or maybe the white wolf's work was done,' Ruby went on. 'Is the man dead?'

'I don't know,' Jake whispered, thinking of Digger, of the howls in the dark mine shaft. 'But I don't think Lucy will have to worry about him any more.'

'That's good, then,' Ruby sighed. 'I see you brought her clothes, from the hollow tree.'

'I thought . . . I hoped, she might need them again,' Jake stammered. He handed the bundle to Ruby, and she stroked the torn and bloody white coat.

'Maybe we'll try and get her a new coat,' Ruby looked at Jake with her kind old eyes. 'This one's seen some tough times. Maybe she'd look nice in something blue.'

Jake felt tears well up in his eyes. He looked back at Lucy. The sheet had slipped off her face and her lips curved up in her familiar smile. Her breath came and went evenly.

'There,' said Ruby. 'It's over. She'll sleep now.' She drew one of Lucy's limp white hands out from under the sheet and kissed it. 'Help me put a blanket on her, Jake,' Ruby said. 'They're a little too heavy for me. Then, we'll let her sleep.'

Jake reached for a soft grey blanket and covered Lucy before they left the room. He wished he had his guitar, so he could play her to sleep in a safe place where there would be no nightmares. He thought of all the music he'd like to write for her.

'You still look hungry,' Ruby said, as they went into the kitchen. 'I have bacon and eggs, and bread for toast, if you know how to cook.'

Jake wanted to kiss her cheek. Now that Lucy was safe, his hunger came back like an express train, screaming through his body.

When he had eaten, Jake and Ruby checked on Lucy again. She was curled in a ball like a child, sleeping hard.

'What will happen to her now?' Jake asked. 'Digger destroyed her shack, and she can't go back to that foster home.'

'I think she will stay here, with me,' Ruby said. 'She is old enough now to say where she wants to live, and I think we should look after each other.'

'Lucy wants to build a bigger place, up on the mountain,' Jake said. 'Maybe I could help. We could make special ramps for your chair . . .'

'I see you are a dreamer,' Ruby laughed softly. 'Maybe a little like your parents.'

Alex picked up her juggling balls and tossed them into the air. 'Well, that's pretty much the end of the story,' she said. 'The authorities did let Ruby officially adopt Lucy, but they didn't stay around here. Lucy had too many bad memories. They went to live in Ruby's old home town.'

'So, Jake never got to help Lucy build a new shack,' Jo said.

'Jake and his parents left the mountain soon after they got back . . . I think they live out west, now.' Alex nodded. 'It turned out the gold ore wasn't rich enough to mine, after all.'

'But you can't just leave the story there!' Jo cried. 'How could Jake and Lucy be separated, after all they'd been through?'

'And what happened about Digger?' Louise shot in her question.

'Digger's body was never found,' Alex shook her head. 'The police believed he was buried by the explosion. Mr Bell believes that he became a werewolf.'

'That fits!' Louise said excitedly. 'Remember how the white wolf nipped him on the hand when he was fastening her to the concrete block? And how Jake thought he looked so hairy and strange just before he fell? He must have already been turning into a werewolf!'

'If you believe in werewolves,' Charlie said. 'I still think the whole thing could just be people's wild imaginations. Up here, in this lonely, cut-off place, you could believe anything!'

'Anyway, if Digger was a werewolf, I sure wouldn't want to meet him,' Jo said. 'He'd be evil, through and through.'

'I'd better put Jake's diary back in the box,' Alex said. 'I wonder why he left it here?' She picked up the metal box and set the diary and the lump of gold ore back on top of the papers.

'Wait a second,' Jo said, reaching for the box. 'Isn't that sheet music?' She pulled a piece of music out of the pile. 'Jake wrote this,' she said excitedly. 'There's his name at the top, and the title: *For Lucy*.'

'And there's an inscription,' Louise pointed.

Someday, when we are together again,
I will play this for you . . .

'Wow,' Charlie sank back on the couch. 'Do you think they ever will get together? How old would they be now?

'Jake must be twenty, and Lucy would be twenty-one,' Jo said. 'At that age, it doesn't matter if the girl is older. And they're both old enough to find each other – if they still want to.'

'Maybe they'll both come back to this cabin some day,' Louise said, 'and that's why Jake left the box here. We'd better put it back.'

They replaced the music and gently closed the box. All four of them sat staring at the fire, thinking about Jake and Lucy.

'Listen,' Alex said, all at once, holding up her hand.

'What? Do you hear wolves again?' Jo said.

'No, I thought I heard a motor noise. Listen! There it is again . . .'

They all heard it now. A high-pitched whine, like an angry bee, from somewhere down the mountain.

'It sounds like snowmobiles,' Alex said. 'I think my parents are on their way.'

They ran to the door, shedding blankets and sleeping bags. When Alex wrenched it open, they crowded into the doorway to look out.

They saw an amazing sight.

The snow had stopped, and the sky was

black velvet – sprinkled with more stars than any of them had ever imagined existed in the universe. They glittered like diamonds, so thick there was hardly any space between.

The sound of snowmobile motors was louder out there.

'I've got an idea,' Alex cried. 'Let's go back inside.'

Forty minutes later, strong headlamps pierced the blackness of the forest and shone into the cabin windows. Heavy skiddoo boots stomped on the cabin floor.

'Alex?' Alex's father called softly.

There was no answer.

'Shhh! They must all be asleep,' came her mother's voice. 'I told you they'd be all right. Look, they've even kept the wood stove going.'

'Phew,' they heard Alex's father sigh. 'That's a relief. I was so worried. I was sure they'd be scared, lonely . . . I guess these kids are a lot tougher than I thought!'

Up in the loft, Alex, Charlie, Louise and Jo smothered giggles in their pillows, and clutched hands in the darkness. Somewhere, out in the forest, a lone wolf howled at the stars.

ORDER FORM

THE SLEEPOVER SERIES
Sharon Siamon

0 340 67276 5	THE SECRET ROOM SLEEPOVER	£3.99	☐
0 340 67277 3	THE SNOWED-IN SLEEPOVER	£3.99	☐
0 340 67278 1	THE HAUNTED HOTEL SLEEPOVER	£3.99	☐
0 340 67279 X	THE CAMP FIRE SLEEPOVER	£3.99	☐
0 340 70904 9	THE SHIVERING SEA SLEEPOVER	£3.99	☐

All Hodder Children's books are available at your local bookshop or newsagent, or can be ordered direct from the publisher. Just tick the titles you want and fill in the form below. Prices and availability subject to change without notice.

Hodder Children's Books, Cash Sales Department, Bookpoint, 39 Milton Park, Abingdon, OXON, OX14 4TD, UK. If you have a credit card, our call centre team would be delighted to take your order by telephone. Our direct line is *01235 400414* (lines open 9.00 am – 6.00 pm Monday to Saturday, 24 hour message answering service). Alternatively you can send a fax on *01235 400454*.

Or please enclose a cheque or postal order made payable to Bookpoint Ltd to the value of the cover price and allow the following for postage and packing:
UK & BFPO – £1.00 for the first book, 50p for the second book, and 30p for each additional book ordered up to a maximum charge of £3.00.
OVERSEAS & EIRE – £2.00 for the first book, £1.00 for the second book, and 50p for each additional book.

Name ....

Address ....

....

....

If you would prefer to pay by credit card, please complete:
Please debit my Visa/Access/Diner's Card/American Express (delete as applicable) card no:

☐☐☐☐ ☐☐☐☐ ☐☐☐☐ ☐☐☐☐

Signature ....

Expiry Date ....